A
Harlequin
Romance

OTHER
Harlequin Romances
by MARY BURCHELL

UNDER THE
STARS OF PARIS

by

MARY BURCHELL

Harlequin Books

TORONTO • LONDON • NEW YORK • AMSTERDAM • SYDNEY • WINNIPEG

Original hard cover edition published in 1954
by Mills & Boon Limited

SBN 373-01964-5

Harlequin edition published April 1976

Printed in Canada

CHAPTER I

ANTHEA walked up the long slope of the Avenue des Champs-Élysées in the clear, cool sunshine of a February afternoon. The sky was that pale, translucent blue which heralds the spring while still retaining the frigid beauty of winter. The trees—so soon to put on the first heavenly green of opening buds—were still leafless and stark. But, in some indefinable way, one knew that the sap was rising, that the life of the year was stirring, and that presently the first intoxicating breath of spring would be wafted along the avenues and boulevards.

Usually the scene enchanted her. Not only the matchless architectural prospect, but also the moving crowds of the Avenue. The stroller, the early tourists, the occasional groups of provincials (too early for many of these) gazing at the sights and feeling that they were seeing life, the busy Parisians themselves, hurrying about their multitudinous affairs, even the smart, sharp-voiced policeman, directing the undirectable traffic.

But today she was walking along with an absorbed and purposeful air. An air which might have deceived anyone into thinking she was bound for an important appointment. The truth was, however, that Anthea had no appointment, no special object in view, no real idea, even, just what she was going to do next. She was deceiving herself just as much as any observer, because she was trying to pretend to herself that she was not frightened and at the end of a road which led nowhere.

In her purse she had exactly fifty francs, which sounds so much more than five pounds but which buys about the same. It was true that the rent of her small room, high up in the tall, old-fashioned house near the École Militaire, was paid until the end of the month. But this

5

room and the fifty francs represented all the security now existing in Anthea's life.

At twenty-one, Anthea Marlowe had experienced rather more emotional ups and downs than usually fall to the lot of anyone so young. Her mother had died when she was sixteen, and Anthea, the sole child of a handsome, popular and successful portrait painter, found herself acting the part of housekeeper in a large, attractive and modern flat, and hostess to an equally large, attractive and modern circle which eddied round her father.

Colin Marlowe was that unusual phenomenon—a socially successful artist. Someone once said of him that he had brought flattery to the finest of fine arts, both on canvas and in the drawing-room. And Anthea—who was not without shrewd powers of judgment—knew that there was much truth in this.

Attractive himself, he liked attractive people round him. Not for him the subtle interest of a face lined with the story of long experience. Gay, good-humoured, tasteful, he had still a touch of the likeable adolescent in his make-up. And while Anthea loved her father, she had no illusions about his reliability as a stay and prop in life.

All the same, the years as his hostess and home-maker had been gay and lovely, if a trifle without purpose.

Then she had met Michael, and almost from that first evening she had known that life had a purpose at last. He was tall and fair and slightly arrogant. The way people always like to think Englishmen are, while, in point of fact, with characteristic contrariness, they usually contrive to be something quite different.

With him too it was a whirlwind affair. He rang her up every day that week, took her out on four evenings, and, driving her home in his car on the Sunday evening, told her that he loved her and wanted to marry her.

"Perfectly delightful!" everyone said. "The ideal match." And—"Made for each other."

For five happy months Anthea thought all this too.

6

The only person who was less than satisfied was her father, and, as he freely admitted, his reserve was based on selfishness pure and simple. (The expression was his own, and he managed to convey the impression that selfishness was something rare and slightly admirable.)

He was naturally reluctant to lose his pretty, efficient and presentable daughter, and often said—with a pathos which he himself secretly admired—that he was a lonely old man now and it seemed as though life were not to hold much more for him.

As he was an extremely well-preserved and attractive forty-eight, no one fell much for the lonely old man story, and as for life not holding much more for him—it was very soon, and rather regrettably, to hold Millicent Edney for him.

No one could deny that she was the type of good-looking, sophisticated, slightly malicious person who always amused him, and Anthea could only hope that this amused interest would stand the test of married life. For herself, she had never liked Millicent, who made a speciality of understanding other people's husbands, but if she were likely to prove the right woman to console her father for her own loss, Anthea was more than willing to make the best of her.

However, hardly had Millicent begun to flash Colin Marlowe's handsome emerald upon her finger when she also began to make it charmingly plain to Anthea that she could not fix her own wedding date too soon for her stepmother-to-be. Nothing nasty—well, frankly nasty —was ever said, of course. It was just that Anthea was made to feel so superfluous that she sometimes wondered what she was doing in her own home.

If her father noticed anything, he affected not to do so. For Anthea—dear and precious though she might be— was already becoming very, very faintly shadowy in outline to him, since she no longer made up part of his own immediate concerns.

Her sense of humour and her admirable tolerance kept

7

Anthea from any open break with Millicent, for, after all, she would herself be marrying in something like six weeks, and it behoved her not to quarrel with her father's choice in that short time.

So Anthea controlled her feelings—even to the extent of going through the whole wedding day with every appearance of good feeling towards Millicent. Then, when the flat was hers while the other two went on their honeymoon, she settled down to the task of sorting out her own belongings and making the final preparations for her marriage.

This was the point at which Michael came to her and told her he had fallen in love with Eve Armoor.

He did not seek to excuse himself. He said he had struggled unavailingly against his feelings and that he deserved anything Anthea liked to call him. But the fact was that he loved Eve, and the only possible course was to tell Anthea the truth and trust to her generosity to release him.

She released him immediately, of course—with a few inadequate words dug out of her frozen consciousness, a few well-sounding platitudes which deceived neither of them but somehow served to fill the ghastly rift which had suddenly been torn in their relationship. Sometimes, as she strove not to recall the scene, she felt that she must have been like someone dropping something which had suddenly become burning hot.

There was no difficulty about the immediate decision. The difficulty came later, when for days and nights on end she could think of nothing but the desperate, aching loss of Michael. Everything she did or thought or planned led straight back to him—and had to be led forcibly away again.

But more cruelly urgent and insistent than any personal tragedy of the emotions is the irresistible march of day-to-day events. And suddenly Anthea was right up against the question of what she was going to do now—where she was to go.

In less than a week her father and Millicent would be returning. And, though her father might be quite content to hear that she was staying at home indefinitely after all, Millicent would be furious. And Millicent being furious in the place which had so swiftly and completely ceased to be home was not something to contemplate calmly.

Anthea felt she could not put enough distance between herself and such a situation. But the state of her finances, and other practical considerations, precluded any very distant flight. Her father had always been lavish and open-handed where housekeeping expenses were concerned. But he demanded in return a very good standard of living and a daughter who was presentable on all occasions. The result was that, although Anthea had lived well, her bank balance was less than a hundred pounds in cold cash. Very much less if she had to settle one or two outstanding matters before making her departure anywhere.

She was determined not to ask her father for assistance. Indeed, she had no intention of being at home when he and his bride returned, for to receive Millicent's sweet-sour commiserations on what had happened was more than she could stand.

And so Anthea had made the decision to go to Paris, which she knew almost as well as she knew London. There she would get a cheap room and teach English, act as companion, nursery governess, receptionist—any of those optimistic-sounding careers which the uninitiated are apt to think exist until they put the issue to the acid test of practical search.

Anthea had been more than two months in Paris by now, but the only work she had found was one week as companion (virtually unpaid) to someone's slightly dotty and very unlikeable great-aunt, and three or four exhausting days caring for a couple of dreadful children who were so revoltingly full of self-expression that she herself could willingly have done some self-expression, of

9

a murderous variety, on her own account.

And so, on this cool, bright February afternoon, she was walking up the Champs-Élysées, looking as though she knew exactly what she was going to do next, and not having a clue.

When she came to the Avenue Georges V she turned along it, thinking that perhaps the slightly quieter scene might give her some sort of inspiration in her dilemma. Then, as she was about to cross the road, she paused to allow a stream of traffic to pass, and, at the same moment, the tall man immediately in front of her stepped back, so that they collided.

"Pardon, mademoiselle!" He turned, raised his hat, and then exclaimed in English, "Why, hello!—I mean—I know you, don't I?"

Anthea was about to say coolly and pleasantly that this opening had grey whiskers on it when she suddenly realized that those curiously light grey eyes and the good line of the cheek and chin were indeed familiar to her.

"Yes, I rather think—— Though I can't remember just where——"

"I can," he said, triumphantly recapturing the memory. "At the Bellingers', last summer. We danced together, and you told me you were engaged to a fellow who designed bridges or something."

So long ago! So cruelly long ago. Almost another world. A world which had securely contained herself and Michael—and no one else who really mattered greatly.

"I remember," she said. "You were over in England for a long weekend, but you told me you worked abroad."

"Diplomatic," he agreed, presumably referring to his status rather than his remark. "I was in Rome at that time, but I've been in Paris for the last few months. Are you staying long or just on a—a shopping trip?"

"He means—am I here to buy my trousseau?" thought Anthea, and wished these things did not still make her wince.

"I am here indefinitely," she stated, and although he could not know it, of course, she really flung down a challenge to fate when she said that.

"Then ˙ hope I may see something of you," he replied. "It's an odd admission to have to make, but never knew your name. Someone just mumbled it at me before we danced. But I'm Roger Senloe. The time we met I was staying with some cousins of mine whom you probably know. The Armoors. The younger one, Eve, has just got engaged recently. Nice chap. Designs bridges or some——" He stopped suddenly, evidently struck by the horrid coincidence.

"Please don't mind." She was sorry for him because he looked much too nice to have said such a thing on purpose. "As a matter of fact, it is the same bridge-designer. My engagement was broken off about a couple of months ago and Michael became engaged to your cousin."

"I couldn't be more sorry or embarrassed," he said, and this was so obviously true that she could not feel quite so raw and hurt as she should have. "You must be Anthea Marlow."

"Yes, I am."

"And out of all the remarks I might have used for light conversation, I had to make that one. Please forgive me."

"But of course."

"And now how do we break off this conversation," she thought, "without drifting on into all sorts of details and complications?"

Something in his glance made her guess that, in spite of everything, he was going to ask about seeing her again. And, with a sudden sensation bordering on panic—a wild desire to escape from anything or anyone who could remind her of the past—she spoke first.

"Look—the traffic is with you. I mustn't keep you. Good-bye."

"You're not coming my way?"

"No. I"—she glanced round—"have an appointment here——" She indicated the fashionable hairdresser's outside which they were standing. "And I'm afraid I am already late."

She smiled at him composedly, made a pleasant little gesture of farewell with her hand, and, resolutely entering the rather imposing doorway, ran up the short flight of steps to the reception desk.

On such minor details do our destinies hang.

It had been Anthea's intention to ask for some imaginary person and then, after the consequent enquiries and discussion, go out into the street again, by which time Eve Armoor's cousin would be safely out of the way. But, as she came up the stairs she saw herself in the large mirror suspended there, and she thought absently,

"I could use a good hair-do at the moment."

Not that she could really think of such luxuries in her present position, of course.

Or could she?

She glanced at the list of charges which hung above the reception desk, in the mood of one who stakes his all on one throw of the dice. And, with a sense of recklessness impossible to explain or justify, she suddenly decided to spend most of her last few francs on having her hair done.

And so, when the receptionist looked up to attend to her, Anthea had, in a few crazy seconds, made her decision.

"You have no appointment, *madame*?" The girl shook her head doubtfully and studied her big ledger with pursed lips. "We are so very busy just now—naturally. But—well, Mademoiselle Claire might manage you."

She called to a dark, vivid, boneless creature in a white smock who was passing, and after a moment or two of discussion, Anthea found herself following Mademoiselle Claire into the vast salon, with wash-basins along one side and a veritable forest of hair-dryers, toilet tables and

12

mirrors disposed about the place.

There was a tremendous amount of chattering and laughing going on and, as Anthea seated herself before one of the basins, she wondered a little wryly why she had supposed that she would find a peaceful hour here. But the scene amused and distracted her. There was some atmosphere of subtle excitement, of tingling anticipation, all around her and, while she could not explain it, in some indefinable way, she felt her spirits begin to rise.

While she waited for Mademoiselle Claire to come to her, she studied her reflection in the mirror and wondered—with the first touch of humour she had been able to bring to the situation—just what it was Eve Armoor had which she lacked.

It was not a bad face, she told herself, dispassionately considering its heart-shaped outlines, and her eyes were good. Dark, large and well-shaped—and the long lashes which fringed them were her own. Her complexion was smooth and creamy, with that faintly golden tint which belongs only to dark-eyed blondes, and while her mouth was a little wide for real beauty, a more objective observer than Anthea herself would have described it immediately as generous.

But perhaps in this hour of depression she had been right to spend her all on her hair. Its golden, silky beauty—in such contrast to her dark eyes—deserved that final crazy gesture, for it shone with all the tender radiance of a good deed in a naughty world.

Even the experienced Mademoiselle Claire paid it an unusual tribute when she returned, for she ran an appreciative—almost a gentle—hand over Anthea's bright head and said in English,

"Very beautiful!"

"Oh, thank you." Anthea smiled at her in the mirror, and then surrendered herself, with a little sigh of contentment, to the strong, expert fingers which seemed in some curious way to smooth away something of the weight of care which rested upon her.

Mademoiselle Claire knew her job. Not until Anthea was seated before one of the dressing-tables, her wet gold hair clinging to her head like a silken cap, did the girl with the comb, the pins and the clips say anything. And then it was only a conventional enquiry about Madame's length of stay in Paris, which could either lead to conversation, if her client so wished, or be briefly answered and succeeded by silence.

"I haven't quite decided how long to stay," Anthea explained. "I have been here about two months." Then, because she had no wish to think—much less talk—of herself, she asked, "Why is it that you're so specially busy and—and full of vitality this afternoon? Your receptionist said that 'of course' you were busy. I wondered why."

"Why, because of the Collections, *madame*. The dress shows, you know. Most of them open next week, and this is the heart of the dress-house district. The mannequins and the *vendeuses*—even the sewing girls—are all excited and all want, of course, to look their best. Some of the most famous mannequins in Paris are here at this moment."

"Is that so?" Anthea looked round with interest. "Tell me who some of them are."

"The girl over there, having a manicure, is from Courrèges," Mademoiselle Claire explained obligingly. "And the dark, very elegant one who is just finished— she is from Balmain."

"And the girl just coming in?" enquired Anthea.

"Ah, she is probably the most famous cover girl in France," Mademoiselle Claire said, on a note of almost possessive pride. "She has been to America. She is what you call free-lance," she added, pleased—and justly so—to show off her excellent English. "Most of the others are on contract to one house or another, and any photographic work or outside modelling they do must be permitted by their employers."

14

"How interesting!" Anthea looked round, studying the types with frank attention. As she did so, she met the equally interested glance of a woman sitting at a nearby table, having the finishing touches put to the exquisitely sleek plaited coronet in which her dark hair was arranged.

Like almost everyone else in the place, she was slender and elegant, and looked immensely alert and vital. As their eyes met she smiled and very slightly inclined her head.

Anthea returned the salutation, hoping she had not looked too shamelessly curious about the scene around her. And then, released from the ministrations of her white-smocked attendant, the woman got up with an air of decision and came across to where Anthea was sitting.

"*Pardon, mademoiselle*"—unlike Mademoiselle Claire, she did not venture on any English—"are you also in the dress world?"

"Unfortunately, no, *madame*." Anthea too spoke in French and smiled the sweet, rather fugitive smile which had once so charmed Michael. "Only an interested observer."

"You say 'unfortunately'. You mean that you would like to be in it?"

"I—don't know. I never thought about it." Anthea gave a slight, surprised laugh. "I have no qualifications for it."

"Except"—the woman turned to Mademoiselle Claire —"that she has the exact colouring—even, I think, almost the exact measurements—of Claudine. I noticed her as soon as she came it. I watched her walk the length of the room, and by nature she walks well."

"So?" There was no mistaking the interest—almost the excitement—in Mademoiselle Claire's voice. "The poor Claudine—she will not be well in time for the Opening?"

"No, of course not. And it is her own fault. She should never have gone driving with that reckless Henri of hers with the Show less than a week away. She broke her leg, you know." And the woman spoke as though the unknown Claudine had only had the leg on loan and had no right to break it.

"It is very sad for her at the beginning of the season," observed Mademoiselle Claire with becoming feeling.

"It is very sad for Monsieur Florian," retorted the other woman sharply. "Eight models created for Claudine—and she was to wear the wedding dress."

"The wedding dress!" Mademoiselle Claire was aghast. So much so that Anthea, who was listening to all this with slight amusement but the most intense interest, could not help asking,

"But surely someone else can wear the wedding dress?"

There was a shocked silence at this. Then Mademoiselle Claire explained gently, as though to a child —and in English so that Anthea would fully comprehend,

"The wedding dress, *madame*, is the last great moment of the Show. As we say, the *grande finale* of the Collection. No one sees it beforehand but the designer and the mannequin who is to wear it——"

"And I also—one day before the Show," put in the other woman austerely, thereby showing that she understood English perfectly well, even if she chose not to speak it very often.

"It is the—the final expression of the designer's art, and must reflect absolutely the personality of the mannequin who wears it. It would be quite, quite impossible for some other type to do justice to it. Only Mademoiselle Claudine, in this case," Mademoiselle Claire said regretfully.

"Or someone who looks very like Claudine," the older woman said.

Anthea met her slightly narrowed gaze in the mirror. And suddenly she felt light and gay and reckless beyond expression. Like someone caught on a wave and swept irresistibly towards a bright but unknown shore.

16

"If I can be of any assistance to you, *madame*, with my colouring—and my measurements," she said, a flash of humour lighting her face with an almost roguish expression, "I shall be very happy to do so."

The other woman flushed slightly, which Anthea took to be a sign of excitement, since she could not imagine that anything ever caused this sophisticated creature embarrassment.

"It is a risk—a gamble," she muttered in rapid French. "But he is a gambler. Perhaps it is less of a gamble than to create and make for Héloïse at this late hour. And she does not look a bride, Héloïse. Young, but not virginal. Why should she?" the woman added in cynical parenthesis.

Then she turned to Anthea and spoke in slow but exact English

"*Mademoiselle*, I am Suzanne Moisant, the *Directrice* of Monsieur Georges Florian, who is, as you know, the greatest dress designer in Paris." She paused here, as though she thought someone might dispute this, in which case she would know how to deal with them.

As Anthea, however, was probably the only client in the place without any passionate local loyalties, she merely inclined her head respectfully and appeared ready to accept this statement at its face value.

"You have heard of our plight," Madame Moisant went on. "It is possible for perhaps four of Claudine's models to be distributed among the other girls, but the other four, including the wedding dress, remain essentially for Claudine or her type. It seems to me that Monsieur Florian would at least want to see you and try you in one of the models.

"If," added Madame Moisant frankly, "you are too fat, or you walk like a camel when you know you are observed, or if in some other way you are impossible, we will thank you for your trouble and part *senza rancor*. If, on the other hand, you are remotely to be considered as a substitute for Claudine, you will have an opportunity

17

of taking part in the most important dress show in Paris next week. Does the idea appeal to you?"

"Enormously," Anthea said, hardly able to keep from breaking into a pæan of joy.

"Then can you come over to the salon as soon as you are ready, please? There is no time to lose."

"I'll be with you in half an hour," Anthea promised, determined to obtain the address from Mademoiselle Claire, rather than admit to Madame Moisant her ignorance of something which, she felt sure, that lady considered should be known to all the world.

Hardly had the *Directrice* of Florian turned her back than Mademoiselle Claire broke out excitedly,

"*Madame*, if this should happen to you! It would be the most dramatic thing of the season. An unknown English girl to wear the wedding dress at the Florian show!"

"I don't really believe it yet," Anthea murmured. "Anyway, I may be quite impossible."

"No, no! It *must* be this way!" the other girl declared. "The story is too good not to be true. I will make you so beautiful that Monsieur Florian will accept you immediately. You will see."

And, indeed, so well did Mademoiselle Claire complete her work that when Anthea emerged from her hands, half an hour later, she certainly looked more exquisitely radiant and lovely than she had done since the first knowledge of Michael's love had provided its own beauty treatment.

Carrying her hat, and conscious that her chestnut brown coat would probably look all wrong from Monsieur Florian's point of view, Anthea left the hairdressing salon, accompanied by the most fervent good wishes of Mademoiselle Claire, and walked the short distance to the imposing, elegant building which had the one word FLORIAN cut in deep capitals in its façade.

On the ground floor was the *boutique* where, as she made her rather shy entry, she was aware of a fascinating

18

array of costume jewellery, scarves, gloves and incredibly expensive-looking dress etceteras.

"Madame Moisant is expecting me," she explained, with far more composure than she felt, and was wafted up the long, mirror-lined staircase to what were evidently rarer regions above.

As she reached the top of the stairs she stepped on to a square landing where there were two or three desks, each with a black-clad *vendeuse* sitting behind it. These women, who did the actual selling of the models, were by no means all young, and the one who came forward to attend to Anthea was an elegant and well-preserved forty-five at least.

Hardly waiting to hear Anthea's repeated request for Madame Moisant, she conducted her along a narrow corridor, carpeted—as were the stairs and landing—in thick soft grey, and ushered her into a room where Madame Moisant, now wearing very smart horn-rimmed spectacles, was also sitting behind a desk.

She removed her spectacles without a word, surveyed Anthea as though from an entirely new angle and said to the *vendeuse* who had accompanied her,

"You see what I mean?"

"But of course, Madame Moisant. It is only a question of the hip measurement."

"Yes. She looks bigger in that coat, of course," Madame Moisant said, making Anthea feel like a well-nourished elephant. "Take off your coat and dress, please, *mademoiselle*, and let us take your measurements."

Anthea obediently removed her outer garments and stood there in her slip while the *vendeuse* expertly flicked a tape-measure around her. She had the impression that both the women held their breath, and she was not sure she was not doing the same. Then Madame Moisant said in the tone of one thanking her Maker,

"Right to a centimetre. I thought I could not be wrong."

"It is a miracle," the *vendeuse* stated reverently, and Anthea blushed and hoped they were not all being rather blasphemous.

"Bring Number Forty-two," Madame Moisant ordered in a tone of emotion, and the *vendeuse* went out, leaving Anthea wondering whether or not Number Forty-two were a person.

When it arrived, however, it turned out to be a dress of stiffened lace in an indescribably beautiful shade of iridescent green—so shining and exquisite that Anthea nearly cried aloud in her surprise and delight.

It was lifted over her head, zipped in sheath-like closeness to her figure, and both women stood back to consider the effect.

"If only she can walk!" Madame Moisant exclaimed, clasping her hands. "Dear heaven, if only she can walk!"

"For all the world as though I were a paralytic," thought Anthea, amused and yet, in some odd way, beginning to catch the infection of excitement. This could mean so much to her—so incredibly much!

"Come along to the salon," Madame Moisant said, and the three of them went out of the room and along another thickly carpeted corridor to a long, light narrow room with a raised centre platform running its full length. At the end where they entered there was a small semi-circular stage, and a side entrance from this, Madame Moisant explained, led to the mannequins' dressing-room.

"Now," Anthea was instructed. "Start from the stage and walk, at a reasonable pace, the full length of the platform, turn—casually, but so that everyone can see all views of the model, and walk back rather more slowly, turn again, and come off at the side of the stage."

Wondering rather frantically what "a reasonable pace" might be, Anthea strove to follow the instructions exactly. But she had to repeat the performance a dozen times before Madame Moisant said,

"She is not quite impossible." And then, to the *vendeuse*, "*Madame*, will you ask Monsieur Florian to come here."

The *vendeuse* disappeared and, turning to Anthea, the *Directrice* said,

"You must not be afraid. You must not mind anything that Monsieur Florian says. He is very nervous just now. A designer's reputation is at stake every time he shows a Collection. And then—for Claudine to do this to us!" Her voice shook slightly as she contemplated afresh the immensity of Claudine's lack of consideration.

Anthea bit her lip and tried not to feel more nervous than ever. Then the *vendeuse* returned, accompanied by a slight, fair-haired man with beautiful hands, thinning hair, and the air of an exhausted and impatient schoolboy.

"It is ridiculous and quite useless," he was saying, in a faintly petulant tone. "Amateur mannequins are the devil at all times, but at the opening of the Collection——"

He stopped suddenly and stared at Anthea, who was standing at the far end of the platform. Then, in a very quiet but completely carrying voice, he said,

"Walk towards me—as though you liked me—and were coming to greet me."

Somehow, that was suddenly so much easier than obeying Madame Moisant's detailed, staccato instructions. Anthea smiled faintly and walked towards him, easily and naturally, and because she was conscious that never in her life before had she worn such a becoming dress, her body moved insensibly with a proud and touching grace.

"Walk away from me and do that again," Monsieur Florian commanded. And Anthea repeated the performance.

"Thank you, *madame*. We shall not need you any more," he said, and unspeakable waves of disappointment engulfed Anthea, until she realized that he had addressed the *vendeuse*. Then he turned to Madame Moisant and said, 'We will see her in the wedding dress.''

"Already?" Even Madame Moisant was startled out of her habitual calm.

"Of course." He looked paler and more exhausted than ever. "If she will not do in the wedding dress, we must begin all over again."

This time it was Madame Moisant who went away, and after a moment, Monsieur Florian said, "Come here, *mademoiselle*."

Anthea came obediently to stand in front of him.

"You understand that, though you are a complete stranger, I am having to trust to your honesty and discretion to a degree I would not use with my closest friends. The secrets of every Collection are guarded— with the utmost jealousy, but the Wedding Dress"— somehow it had acquired capitals when spoken of in that quiet, tired, urgent voice—"is the most closely guarded secret of all. I have no choice but to share this with you now. Today is Friday. The Collection will not be shown until Tuesday. Can I rely on you to guard this secret as faithfully as we do ourselves?"

"Of course," Anthea said gravely. "I promise you, *monsieur*, that whether you engage me or not, I shall know nothing of the two dresses I have seen when I go out of here."

"*Bon!*" He turned away and said nothing more to her until Madame Moisant returned, carrying over her arm what looked to Anthea something like a cloud of morning mist, sparkling with the dews of dawn.

"Come!" she said peremptorily, and led Anthea into the empty dressing-room behind the little stage, where she expertly peeled off the green lace dress and, with the deftest and lightest of touches, arrayed her in the fabulous wedding gown.

Then, and only then, did it come over Anthea, with a wave of ironic bitterness, that she was being given the

22

exquisite shadow in place of the precious substance. The most beautiful wedding dress in the world—but no wedding, no Michael!

She started to say something confused about not being able to go on with it after all, but, with a purposeful air, the other woman thrust her out on to the small stage. At the end of the long platform Monsieur Florian stood, and as she hesitated, he said,

"Come, *mademoiselle*. And remember you are a bride."

She found herself walking forward. She knew that her smile must be tremulous and her dark eyes misty with unshed tears. But the age-old compulsion of the show which must go on was for the first time upon her. She walked towards Monsieur Florian as she would have walked towards Michael if things had been different.

"Bravo, bravo!" she heard the Frenchman say softly. "Almost too much heart, too much humanity. But, my God, if she can do that each time!"

Then he turned to Madame Moisant, hovering in the background and said briskly,

"That will do. Take the dress from her. Engage her on the usual terms. She will wear all Claudine's models except Nineteen and Seventy-four, which are too sophisticated. The show for the work-girls tomorrow will give her something of a rehearsal. Now all we have to do is to name her."

"My name is Anthea," said Anthea timidly.

"Anthéa?" He gave it its French pronunciation. "Possible, but it is unlucky to use your real name. With that hair like a flat halo she should have the name of a saint or an angel."

Incongruously, Anthea thought of the phrase, "Michael and all the angels", and at the same moment Monsieur Florian said,

"The archangel, of course! Gabriel. Let her be Gabrielle." Then he nodded to her briefly and went away.

So bewildered and excited was Anthea by all that had

happened to her that she had some difficulty in concentrating on the details of her subsequent interview with Madame Moisant. But she emerged from it with a confused impression that she was to earn a salary that would keep her in very reasonable comfort if she continued to live simply. In addition to this she would have a commission on each sale of the various models she was to display.

What was quite clear in her mind was the fact that she must be at the salon at half-past nine the following morning, for further coaching, and that there would be a private showing of the Collection for the benefit of the work-girls.

"It is not often done," Madame Moisant explained. "But it is a good idea. Started by Balmain," she admitted grudgingly. "The girls always complained that they did all the work but never saw the finished Collection. This year they were promised their own show, provided they finished the work by the Saturday before the opening. Now you had better go home, Gabrielle"—she smiled suddenly and attractively, "rest and don't over-eat."

With so little money in her purse, Anthea followed out this advice perforce, returning to her small attic room with the feeling that she had lived through a month's experiences since last she left it.

The next day she presented herself at Florian's, with outward composure and inward trepidation. This time she was introduced to her fellow mannequins—all occupying the crowded dressing-room behind the salon, chattering, laughing, complaining and, in one case, weeping copiously.

Most of them accepted her with casual friendliness, though in one or two cases with a slight reserve, due either to her being English or of amateur status—Anthea was not quite sure which. The weeping one made her position quite clear in the first five minutes by referring (in French, it was true, but with great distinctness) to "clumsy amateurs".

This Anthea discovered was Héloïse. And the furious tears, she learned to her astonishment, were due simply to the fact that she was not, after all, to have a new wedding dress created specially for her. The accident to Claudine had led her to believe that this honour might be hers, and now the "clumsy amateur" had spoilt it all. As Anthea was soon to find, a disappointment or slight of much smaller proportions than this was quite sufficient to reduce most of them to tears or a display of temperament.

"Don't be a child, Héloïse. You have the most dramatic model in the whole collection," Madame Moisant told her sharply. "And three, at least, of the best selling ones. The wedding dress will not be sold many times, whereas——"

"As though money were everything, *madame!*" cried Héloïse, wrapping her dressing-gown around her with a gesture of scorn and rage. At which Madame Moisant uttered a cynical "Ha-ha!" and went about her own affairs.

The show that evening was an exciting and even curiously moving occasion. Carrying their work stools, about two or three hundred sewing-girls crowded into the salon, along the corridor and out on to the landing. The mannequins, in high good humour, put on the show with as much care and finesse as if they had been displaying the models to the first buyers of Europe, and the applause—divided with the strictness of local loyalties—showed quite plainly which girls had been responsible for the production of each model.

Anthea, as she emerged for the first time—in a little black suit with white broadtail collar and cuffs—was secretly shaking with nervousness. But from the group on her left came a concentrated and deeply satisfied, "*Comme elle est jolie!*" and she found herself being rapturously applauded by the girls who had made the suit.

She wondered if clever Madame Moisant had arranged to have them placed just there. And sustained by the first uninhibited applause she had ever earned, she made the tour of the salon, corridor and landing in admirable style.

The whole occasion was like a successful dress rehearsal of a play. And now, ahead of them all, loomed the ordeal of the opening "performance". Everyone went home that weekend with the sole intention of relaxing and making ready for the great event. Only Monsieur Florian looked as though he could not relax until Tuesday was safely over.

On Tuesday everyone indulged in a few "first-night" nerves. Everyone was either abnormally gushing or unpardonably nervy and rude. Héloïse stared so balefully at Anthea that, against her better judgment, Anthea ventured to speak.

"I'm terribly sorry you were so disappointed over the wedding dress," she said. "But I'm sure your turn will come another year, and none of us could wish poor Monsieur Florian the frightful strain of creating an entirely new design at this late hour. Incidentally— if it's of any interest to you—I needed that job so desperately that I can hardly believe even now that I have it."

Héloïse flickered her long, curiously gold-tipped lashes, and then unexpectedly threw her arms round Anthea and kissed her emotionally.

"You must forgive me," she said. "I am wicked and jealous. But now I am sorry and we will be friends, is it not?"

"Why, of course," Anthea agreed, greatly relieved, and somehow contriving to hide the fact that she was also a good deal amused.

But, as she moved away, Odette—the infinitely elegant, faintly tragic-looking girl who showed all the most sophisticated models—murmured,

"Like hell you will be friends! Be careful. She is wicked and jealous, as she says—but not sorry."

Anthea was a good deal disturbed by this, but there was no time now to sort out the internal politics of the

26

dressing-room. Already the invited guests were beginning to arrive, while the final masses of flowers—many of them ill-wishing tributes from rival designers—were being set in place.

The mannequins were strictly confined to the dressing-room, where most of the models to be shown already hung in place, and presently Madame Moisant came in, with a typed list in her hand.

"It is traditional that I announce the models cn the opening day," she explained good-humouredly, seeing Anthea look interested. "Also at the Press Show and when the first buyers come. I stand here"—she indicated a small, curtained space at the side of the stage—"and through here I can see the salon and the reaction of the audience. Do you want to have a look?"

Obligingly, she stepped aside so that Anthea could peep through the small aperture arranged in the curtains.

It was a fascinating spectacle—rows of chairs crowded either side of the raised platform, and everyone with an air of expectancy again reminiscent of the first night of an important play. Among the audience Anthea recognized several well-known figures in the theatrical and social world. And then, as her gaze travelled slowly back to those nearest her, she gave a slight gasp and felt the blood rush from her face to her suddenly thumping heart.

For there, in the second row, waiting to enjoy the spectacle, sat Eve Armoor. On one side of her was the cousin Anthea had met in the Avenue Georges V. On the other, only a few feet away from Anthea, sat Michael, looking faintly bored.

CHAPTER II

FOR a moment Anthea stood stock-still, her hand gripping a fold of the curtain. Then she said, in a small choked voice,

"*Madame*, I am not well. I—I can't go on."

It was the idiom of her world. The pleasant, easy, social world, where one could, if one simply must, escape from an unbearable situation with a conventional excuse.

But it was not the idiom of Madame Moisant's world.

"Stop being a fool," she said sharply. "This is no time to be ill. If you are not well, you will pretend that you are. You are just nervous. We all are. Me!—do you suppose I feel well at this moment? Monsieur Florian—how well do you suppose he feels, smiling there to his enemies as well as his friends, and knowing that half the flowers sent here today would more gladly have been sent for his funeral? You are perfectly well and you will behave not like an idiot. No hysterics, please, or I shall slap your face with my own hand. It is not a moment for cold water with so many models around," she concluded with a dry laugh.

During this speech—delivered rapidly, in Madame Moisant's most energetic style—Anthea had been groping after her self-control. She had known from the first word that there was no escape. She was as securely caught in this nightmare as if she were dreaming the whole thing and could not wake up. Indeed, that was rather how it felt.

Then, at the mention of Monsieur Florian, some sort of desperate, proud calm came to her, and the ghastly tightness in her chest relaxed so that she found she could breathe almost naturally again. He had trusted her. He had trusted her to wear the flower of his Collection

28

—not to betray his secrets—not to let him down in any way. He had even said he was showing her a degree of trust he would not show his closest friends. And was she to walk out on him now—even if it were possible to do so—just because a man who thought her less than Eve Armoor was sitting the other side of that curtain?

"It's all right," she whispered a little huskily to Madame Moisant. "It's past. I—I just panicked for a moment, as you said."

"Good! All is well now." And, with a sure instinct for the passing of a crisis, Madame Moisant turned from her as though she had ceased to exist, hissed for silence among the excited mannequins, imperiously beckoned to Odette, and then, taking up her position, spoke a few introductory words, first in French and then in English, which immediately silenced all chatter in the room beyond.

"*Numéro cinq*. Numbaire fife," announced Madame Moisant. Odette stepped nonchalantly out upon the small stage. The Show had begun.

Anthea stood there in her black suit with the white broad-tail collar—the first model she was to display—counting off on her fingers those that went before her. It was confusing, because the numbers had no natural sequence. Only the gesture from Madame Moisant called each girl in turn to the narrow point of exit.

But the moment was approaching. Now. Next—after Héloïse who was stepping forth so confidently in her insolent lacquer-red *tailleur* and drawing the first applause from the audience beyond that curtain.

Madame Moisant, peering through the small aperture, smiled briefly and triumphantly. Then, as Héloïse gave her final twirl and departed along the corridor which also served as part of the salon on this crowded occasion, she announced firmly,

"*Numéro dix-huit*. Numbaire eighteen."

Gabrielle—she was Gabrielle at this moment, not

29

Anthea—stepped out into the ring of light. She smiled faintly at everyone and at no one, as she had been taught to do, and walked "at a reasonable pace" up the long platform, passing within a few feet of Michael and Eve, affecting not to hear the slight gasp from one—or was it both?—of them.

At the end, she turned, with that particular swinging motion which "spread" the line of her skirt without destroying it, and started her journey back. It was more difficult this time not to see them. They were within her natural range of vision for a much longer time. But, somehow, she looked past Michael—she looked past Eve—and then her distant gaze faltered. She could not quite manage to look past the cousin. Their eyes met. There was the faintest smile of recognition.

Then she was past, had executed her final swing round, and was out and along the corridor where no ghosts from the past awaited her.

The worst moment was over, she told herself. She had administered—and withstood—the first shock. Anything which followed was merely repetition. And repetition tended to dull, rather than intensify, any emotion.

Until, of course, one came to the high point of the afternoon. The moment when she should step forth in the wedding dress.

She must not think about it beforehand—must not linger on the horrible, ironic fact that she would be parading before Michael in a wedding gown—without the wedding. There were other dresses to show first, and she must remain calm and smiling and mistress of the occasion.

As the afternoon went on, the applause grew more frequent and more prolonged. The subtle wind of success began to blow once more through the salon of Florian. The "dead" two months before the launching of the Show were at an end. Incredibly crowded and exciting weeks lay ahead.

Tension among the mannequins was relaxing, though the watchfulness of Madame Moisant remained the same. Smiles came more easily now, and all the hurried, eager comments in the dressing-room were happy ones. Everyone was in a superbly well-wishing mood all at once, and rivalries and slights were forgotten.

Most of the girls had begun to pick out their favoured customers in the audience by now, and they allowed themselves a personal smile as they passed—and many comments backstage. Since this seemed to be the natural order of things, Anthea—now incredibly calm and mistress of herself—actually contrived to give Michael a smile when she came out wearing her fourth model. Why not? To use the familiar and horribly incongruous phrase, they had "parted friends", had they not?

He seemed to think so too, for he smiled in return, quite coolly, and inclined that handsome head of his. After all, it was not the fault of either of them that Eve had chosen to come here to buy some of her trousseau. Perhaps, even, it was the wedding gown in which she was interested!

At this thought, Anthea had difficulty in choking back a bitter, hysterical little laugh, and, realizing suddenly the danger of indulging in any personal thoughts at this moment, she deliberately made her mind blank and became Gabrielle once more.

It was very near the end now. Héloïse, in the fabulous dress of ostrich fronds, was making the rounds to the sound of unbroken applause. It seemed that the pitch of delighted excitement could hardly mount higher. Surely even the wedding gown could not compete with this sensation.

And then Monsieur Florian himself had come in and across to Anthea, already being arrayed in the cloudy miracle of the final model.

The other mannequins, who had crowded round in voluble admiration, scattered before the *chef*, so that Anthea and Monsieur Florian were left isolated, but, even so, he spoke in English, to make their conversation even more private.

"I want you," he said, "to look just as you did the afternoon I tried you out. Not too radiant—a little tremulous too, as though tears are not so far off. Think that the man you wish to marry is really there before you and——"

"He is," Anthea said baldly, before she could stop herself.

"Eh?" For a moment the Frenchman looked startled.

"I mean"—she suddenly could not keep any of it back—"he is sitting out there now, with the girl he preferred to me." Then, seeing the dismay in the watchful eyes which never left her face, she went on, "It's all right. I'll manage. It's nobody's fault. Just the way life sometimes is. I won't—let you down."

And, greatly to his credit, at the height of his Show, Monsieur Florian spared a thought for feelings other than his own.

"*Pauvre petite*," he said, in that low-pitched, curiously compelling voice of his. "Be brave for five minutes longer. Forget any man who can be so stupid, and look as you will look one day for his lucky successor."

She laughed at that. She actually found herself laughing. And, just for a moment, she saw the clouds of her wretchedness part and beyond them was the bright gleam of a yet unknown radiance. It was sheer imagination, of course, but such are the flashes of imagination which carry us through the worst crisis.

In a hush that could be felt, Madame Moisant made her final announcement, and Anthea stepped out on to the stage—a girl going to meet her future, a bride going to meet her bridegroom, and around her the touching, lovely aura of all youth going with mingled hope and fear to meet the unknown.

For a moment the almost breathless hush held. Then, as she seemed almost to float forward in the cloud of beauty that was Florian's inspiration, the whole place

32

broke into clapping and—incredibly—cheering. She was aware that people had actually risen to their feet, that exclamations were breaking out on every side. But there were only two voices she distinguished as she slowly made her way back.

"That's the dress I want!" she heard Eve Armoor say, on a note of steel-like determination. And Michael's voice, harsh suddenly, as Anthea had never heard it before, said curtly, "You can't possibly. Anything but that!"

Oh, sweet, sweet moment of triumph! Not only for the cheers and praise on every hand. But because she still had the power to move Michael to the depths. Move him to such an extent that he curtly refused his Eve something, because it was too closely and intimately associated with herself.

None of the rest of her triumphal progress surpassed that one giddy moment, but she completed the full round at that slow, floating pace, and returned to the dressing-room to receive Monsieur Florian's curt "Bravo! It was well done," before he went out to acknowledge the congratulations of his departing guests, or linger sociably with those who wanted to hear and see more.

Madame Moisant accorded her a nod of extreme approval. Though her comment reflected more credit on herself than on Anthea.

"I knew I could not be mistaken," she said complacently. "It was a good choice, though you are but amateur. In this way the Show was saved." And she hurried away to speak to the most favoured clients of all.

Relieved of the weight and responsibility of the wedding dress, Anthea felt suddenly tired after all the strain. She stretched her arms above her head, in a luxurious moment of respite, and looked around.

Odette was slipping into one of the suits which was obviously to be a best-seller of the show. Héloïse, very tiresomely, was sitting sulking once more in a corner. All the other girls were busy in other parts of the building.

"Oh dear," whispered Anthea to Odette. "What's the matter with her now?"

Odette glanced over indifferently.

"The applause," she explained succinctly.

"But she had loads of applause!" Anthea exclaimed, bewildered. "I thought they would never stop, when she showed the ostrich feather dress."

"But you had more," Odette replied simply. "They cheered the wedding gown.'

"And—and does it matter so much?"

"*Et comment!*" explained Odette with a laugh. "Me, I am the only generous-minded one here," she went on with frank self-appraisal. "I can bear to have others applauded. It is strange, but this is the way I am built." And she gave Anthea the tragic smile which covered a singularly contented disposition and drifted away.

Anthea was just trying to decide whether or not to try some overture towards Héloïse when Madame Moisant came in and applied her own particular brand of spur.

"Come, stupid one!" she exclaimed cheerfully to the scowling, lovely Héloïse. "Come out of your corner and your sulks. You are to be photographed in Number Sixty-two—the lacquer-red *tailleur*. Fortunate girl! You are the first to be photographed. But hurry, hurry! It is for *En Avant*, and one does not keep them waiting."

The effect on Héloïse was magical. She was smiling long before Madame Moisant had finished, and was already getting ready to insinuate herself into Number Sixty-two.

"To be chosen for photographing—that is the most subtle compliment of all," she informed Anthea.

"I'm sure it is," Anthea said, wondering if she were now supposed to dissolve into tears of chagrin. "I hope it's a colour photograph. Your skin looks marvellous against that red."

"True," the other girl agreed, giving Anthea a very odd glance, as though she were trying to decide what ulterior meaning lay behind those flattering words.

Then Anthea was called to display the green lace, and for a while she saw no more of Héloïse.

She emerged from the dressing-room with a certain degree of trepidation. It was, after all, possible that Eve had lingered to do some immediate ordering—and even remotely possible that Michael had stayed behind too, in the hope, or at least intention, of seeing herself.

But there was no sign of either of them. Neither the person she most feared, nor the one she most hoped, to see. Anthea was merely called on to display the green dress for a curiously unsophisticated young débutante who nearly wept with excitement and delight at the thought of so beautiful a creation being hers.

The last few hours flew past, Anthea being called on several times to show her models, and by the time six o'clock approached they were sufficiently tired and drained of excitement to welcome the hour of release. It was just at this point that Héloïse—who had been called for further photographing outside the building— came to Anthea and said, quite agreeably,

"Your beau is waiting for you outside in his car."

"My——? *Who* did you say was waiting for me?"

"The good-looking man in the second row who smiled at you," explained Héloïse, who had apparently missed nothing either at the moment of one of her own exits, or else by looking through some vantage point from the dressing room.

"Is that so?" Anthea tried to speak very calmly, but she knew she had gone pale.

So he was waiting for her! Michael was waiting for her outside, just as though everything were not over— and more than over—between them. For some reason or other, he felt he must see her—speak to her, if only once again. Wildest apprehension and joy and sheer devouring curiosity assailed her.

But if only he waited long enough! If only she were not delayed beyond the limit of his patience and deter-

35

mination! Everything might well depend on that, and though his determination was great, she remembered, his patience was not.

No one was speaking yet of leaving. Several of the mannequins seemed to have work—photographic work and further display—which would apparently take them on almost into the small hours of the morning. But they were ones like Odette, who were well-known personalities in their own right. For herself it was surely not unreasonable to hope that she might escape almost on time.

And then rescue appeared in the shape of Madame Moisant.

"There is no need for you to stay more," she told Anthea. "Go home now and rest well. Tomorrow morning is the Press Show. For this we must be our best and our most gracious, for we hate and fear them more than all. Then in the afternoon come the international buyers. You have been a good girl and done very well. But don't let a little success go to your head. It was the dress which made the sensation, not you."

"Of course," Anthea agreed. She would have agreed to anything in her happiness over her release, and, in any case, she firmly believed that it *was* Monsieur Florian's dress which had been the success. She only had had the good fortune to wear it.

Losing no time, she slipped into her street clothes—which looked strangely undramatic after the creations she had been putting on and off all the afternoon—and prepared to go.

At the very last moment Monsieur Florian himself came into the dressing-room and, for a dreadful moment, Anthea thought that his imperious "Mademoiselle Gabrielle" was going to spell fatal delay. However, it seemed that he only wished to add a few words to the very brief praise he had been able to give her at the end of the Show.

"It went well, *mademoiselle*, and I have to thank you

for your part in it," he said, with that brilliant but fleeting smile of his. "But if you helped to make my Show, it is also true that my Show has helped to make you. Tomorrow we will have you photographed in the wedding dress, and if you photograph as well as you look in real life, you should have a career before you."

"Oh, Monsieur Florian, thank you!" She too smiled and then held out her hand to him. After a moment he took it and held it briefly in his thin, beautiful fingers.

"The—man who mattered, was he impressed?" Monsieur Florian enquired, with a flash of sentimental curiosity rare in a Frenchman.

"I don't know, *monsieur.*" She glanced down for a moment, then her dark eyes flashed up again in an almost mischievous glance. "But he is waiting outside in his car now."

"*Eh bien!*" Monsieur Florian laughed heartily for once and lapsed into his own language. "I must not keep you, *mademoiselle.* It seems his second thoughts may not have served him so well. But be sure that *your* second thoughts are wise ones. Good luck!" And he left her for more important matters.

She ran down the stairs, calling out "Good night" to one or two of the *vendeuses* as though she had been there for years, and then through the *boutique*, where someone sprayed her automatically with some delicious perfume reserved for this great day.

Finally she was past even the grandly uniformed commissionaire and out into the sharp, clear, exhilarating cold of the late February evening. Ranged along the kerb were several imposing-looking cars, and for a moment her glance travelled over them in doubt.

But her appearance must have been long awaited, for, even as she hesitated, the door of a black car close at hand swung open and she saw a tall figure move over from the driving seat as though he were about to get out.

With a sensation of joy which no resentment nor disil-

37

lusionment could dim, she ran across the pavement towards the car.

Then she stopped short, feeling as though the ground had dropped away in front of her. For the man who got out of the car was not Michael at all. It was Eve Armoor's cousin, whose very name escaped her in this moment of abysmal disappointment.

"Hello," he said, smiling down at her. "I was beginning to wonder if they kept you in all night after a jamboree of this sort. But I decided that if you ever did escape you'd probably be pretty fagged and hungry after all that standing around, and I though maybe you might like me to take you some quiet place for dinner."

It was a second or two before his meaning penetrated, because suddenly all her thought processes had slowed down so that she could take in nothing but the fact that Michael had not been waiting for her, after all.

"Why—how kind of you," she heard herself say, in a very creditable, conventional tone. "But I don't think I——" She stopped, aware all at once that she was dog-tired and ravenous, and that, though the bottom had dropped out of her world all over again, the offer of a good meal was not to be despised in the lean week that would be hers until she earned her first pay packet.

"Yes, I *am* hungry," she asserted. "Hungry and flat out with weariness. If you'll really be so sweet as to take me somewhere to eat, and not expect me to be wildly entertaining and scintillating, then I'll remember you with gratitude for the rest of my days."

He laughed, taking the figure of speech for the light absurdity it was. But, in point of fact, as he handed her into the car and took his seat beside her, she did at least remember what his name was. Which was a help if she was to spend even part of the evening with him.

He didn't ask her where she wanted to go. He seemed to sense that she wanted no demands made upon her—not even that she should have to make so small a decision. But he drove off with an air of decision towards the left bank of the river, and it was some minutes before he spoke at all. Then he said, in a matter-of-fact tone,

"It was quite a surprise, seeing you there this afternoon."

She laughed slightly, trying hard not to make it either hurt or bitter in tone.

"It was quite a surprise seeing you," she told him drily. "All of you."

"Yes—I'm sorry. I hadn't the faintest idea you worked there, of course, or I'd never have arranged for them to come."

"Oh—it was your arrangement, was it?"

"In a way—yes. They—my cousin is in Paris for a week or so to do some shopping——" He stopped, kicked himself, she rather thought, and began again. "You know how it is. All the girls think of Paris and dress shows as being synonymous."

"It's quite all right," she said wearily—almost gently. "I quite understand that she is here to buy her trousseau and probably her wedding dress. It gave her a real kick this afternoon to realize that she might wear in actual fact the wedding dress I was just showing as a model. Only Michael doesn't want it that way, does he?"

There was a short silence, then the man beside her said, "You've got it all taped so accurately that I don't know it's much good my adding anything. Except that she won't have that particular dress, if it's of any importance to you."

"Did Michael insist?"

"Well, he was pretty emphatic. And I managed to make her see she'd be a damned fool if she tried to drive him."

"Thank you," Anthea said. "It would have been—hard being the mannequin, in the circumstances."

"That's what I thought," he agreed drily. And then, again in that matter-of-fact tone, "You're darned good

39

at your job. Most of those girls just look like lovely dummies. But you're real all the time."

She laughed at that, accountably flattered as well as pleased.

"Tell me some more things like that," she said almost gaily. "You're talking to the most inexperienced mannequin in Paris. It's the first show I've ever done."

"I don't believe it!" He glanced at her, incredulous, amused and admiring.

"It's true." She felt reckless, suddenly, and light-hearted—or was it light-headed? "I'll tell you the whole story presently, when we've had some food."

"Agreed," he said, and drew the car to a standstill just round the corner from a small, gay restaurant where one could look out across the water to the soaring lines of Notre-Dame.

And until they had disposed of their reviving *consommé*, with thin crisp batons of bread to accompany it, and the succulent duckling piquantly and sharply dressed with sections of orange, he determinedly kept the conversation on light and impersonal subjects.

Then, over coffee and the deliciously creamy dessert which Anthea shamelessly selected, in defiance of Madame Moisant's precepts, he said,

"Now tell me how you came to be a mannequin and the Success of the Show."

"I don't know that I'd claim to be that, exactly," Anthea murmured.

"Of course you were!" Even your little feathered friend couldn't compète, for all her hip-waggling."

"Oh——" Anthea had to laugh at this description of Héloïse. And she laughed again a good many times, she found, over the story of her incredible escapade. He laughed too, giving her the impression that she was being very witty and entertaining, though she had thought when she first came out that she would not be able to utter anything but strained platitudes.

Presently she realized that he was not the only one

who was enjoying himself. Whether it was the good food she had eaten, or the excellent red wine which had accompanied it, whether it was anything to do with finding herself financially in quiet waters after weeks of strain and anxiety, she could not have said. Perhaps it was something of all three. But the plain fact was that she was extracting a great deal of amusement and pleasure from this evening with Eve Armoor's cousin.

It was with a little sigh of regret that she finally said, "I'm afraid I should go now. We're supposed to get all the rest we can for further endurance tests ahead."

He called for their bill immediately, without making any attempt to prolong the evening—a mark of real consideration which she counted to his credit. All he did say, to mark his keen enjoyment, was that he hoped she would agree to their doing this again.

She hesitated just a second and he grinned at her and said,

"I can't help being Eve's cousin, you know. You *could* take the view that compensations, rather than penalties, were called for."

She laughed a little reluctantly and bit her lip. But she ended by saying that she would be very happy to come out with him another time.

He drove her home then, in spite of her protests that she could go by Métro if he would drop her at the nearest station. And, as they neared the long street of old-fashioned houses in which Anthea lived, he said,

"I want to ask you something, but don't be either hurt or insulted, will you?"

"Oh"—she winced apprehensively—"nothing about Michael, please!"

"Good lord, of course not! What sort of interfering ass do you think I am? No—the fact is that, though you told me a most gay and entertaining story of how you came to be acting as a mannequin in Florian's salon, I'm somehow left with the impression that you must be darned short of money until your first week's or month's

41

salary comes in. Are you, Anthea? And will you let me—in the most respectable and Diplomatic Service manner possible—make good that shortage?"

"Oh—Roger——" She hadn't really meant them to be on Christian names terms quite so quickly, but it was difficult to be formal with anyone so completely tactful and understanding. "It's terribly nice of you"—she actually patted his arm—"and if I were absolutely desperate I would let you. But I'm paid at the end of the week, and provided I'm very, very careful——"

"But do you have to be very, very careful, now an alternative is offered?" he wanted to know.

"I'd rather, if I can manage it."

"But if you can't, will you tell me? I don't like the idea of your starving in a Paris attic, like some operatic heroine." In spite of his laughing words, his tone was serious.

"All right. I promise that, if I can't manage to eat reasonably well without help, I'll let you lend me some," she said sincerely. "And whether I have to accept the offer or not, I'll never, never forget that you made it, Roger, and in such nice terms."

"My dear girl, I don't know what you're talking about. Just a matter of common sense and book-keeping."

She laughed softly.

"Oh, no. It's of a piece with everything else you've done and said. I simply can't imagine why you've gone out of your way to be so kind to a virtual stranger."

"No?" He gave her an odd, smiling little glance, and then suddenly he looked rather grim and somehow older than she had supposed him to be. "You can set it down to the account of 'fellow-feeling', Anthea. I too was turned down flat by the girl I was crazy about. I know pretty accurately what you've been feeling the last few months."

CHAPTER III

ANTHEA looked at Roger Senloe, and for the first time she saw him as a person. Not just Eve Armoor's cousin. Not just the man who had providentially taken her out and distracted her thoughts on this most difficult evening. But as someone in his own right. Someone who also had suffered a searing experience—and come out of it a slightly cynical but curiously likeable person.

She saw, as though these details appeared for the first time, that his eyes, besides being light and bright, were penetrating, that his features were strongly marked and significant, and that his expression was that of a man who knew what he wanted and nearly always got it.

Not quite always. Some girl—*the* girl—had turned him down, and in circumstances that had hurt enough to give him an uncanny insight into her own experience.

"I'm so very sorry," she said quietly. "Was it—a long time ago?"

"Not long enough," he told her with a slight grimace.

He had stopped the car now before her house, but she still sat there, staring thoughtfully ahead, as though she saw more than the quiet, empty street.

"It's the way it keeps on coming back that makes it so difficult, isn't it?" she said slowly. "You think you have yourself in hand, and that it will really be better soon, and then something happens which puts you back just where you were, and you have to start being heroic all over again. Only suddenly you know you're not even being heroic. Just foolish and rather pitiable. And then that hurts most of all."

"Poor child," he said, but it sounded more bracing, somehow, than Monsieur Florian's "*pauvre petite.*"

"You've had a worse packet than I. At least I had my

work and no anxiety about being able to stand on my own feet in that sense."

She glanced up then, the wistfulness of her smile suddenly banished—or almost so—in a flash of roguishness.

"I can stand on my own feet too, after today," she told him. "That's why I'd rather not take anything if I can help it. Somehow, as Gabrielle I can face the world. Even—even Michael and Eve. I've proved it. Haven't I?—haven't I?" And suddenly her voice broke a little because of the rush of almost childish panic and the frantic necessity for reassurance.

"You did about the bravest thing I've ever seen this afternoon," Roger Senloe told her, and his matter-of-fact tone steadied her as nothing else could have done. "You'll probably never again have to do anything so hard. Remember that."

"Oh, I can't tell you what you do to my morale when you say something like that!" She managed to smile almost brilliantly again.

"And I can't tell you what it does to my morale to take out the most sensational mannequin in Paris," he retorted lightly.

"That's not very accurate, you know," she protested with a laugh.

"It's going to be," he assured her. "And before you get dated up by all the other fellows is it a bargain that we go out together sometimes, for the benefit of our respective morales? After all, neither of us will ever have to pretend with the other. We know we're a bit disillusioned and a bit cowardly about certain patches in our past. It gives us a sort of mutual understanding."

She laughed a little, but the odd idea appealed to her. Like that other crazy idea which had landed her eventually in Florian's.

"All right," she said. "It's a bargain—for the future. But now it is really good night—and a thousand thanks."

He told her where she could get in touch with him if

44

she needed to do so, and then waited while she took out her key and opened the great heavy door of the house where she lived. Then, with a final wave, he drove off, leaving her to step into the large, gloomy hall of a house which had once known magnificence, but so long ago that there were hardly any traces of it left.

Anthea took the creaking lift to the fifth floor and then ascended the final flight of steps to the humble, remote level which the lift refused to serve. As in so many continental apartment houses, these top rooms were really intended for the maids who worked in the households below. But few households in this type of house could indulge in such luxuries now, so one could sometimes rent from the householder concerned one of these rooms.

For a fairly modest monthly sum, Anthea had a small, not unattractive room with a sloping ceiling and a window which looked out over the roofs of Paris to the great circular dome of the Invalides, that noble structure where Napoleon, who menaced Europe, and Foch, who a hundred years later did much to save Europe, sleep side by side.

She slept herself that night, dreamlessly and well, in spite of the fact that two ghosts from the past had risen to confront her at the moment when she would have said she could least cope with them.

The next morning she was up in good time and walked to work, in cold but brilliant sunshine, along the Avenue Bosquet, across the Pont de l'Alma and up the Avenue Georges V. Everything to her looked bright and gay. The buildings, the shining windows, the pale, clear sky, the enchanting articles arranged seductively in shop windows—even the faces of the people she passed. But perhaps that was just because of her new and hopeful mood.

As she arrived at the entrance to Florian's the great designer was himself alighting from his car, and at the doorway he came up with her.

"Monsieur Florian! Monsieur Florian!" a voice cried urgently behind them, and instinctively they both turned. As they did so, a man standing a few feet away from them clicked a camera triumphantly, cried fervently, "*Merci, monsieur!*" and, leaping into a car which was standing at the kerb with its motor running, was driven off at great speed.

For a moment Florian scowled. Then he shrugged and said,

"Good morning, *mademoiselle*. I hope no one who sees that photograph thinks I designed the coat you are wearing."

"It's rather a nice coat," Anthea replied with spirit.

"But I do not design 'rather nice coats'," Florian replied with a dry smile, and entered the portals he had made famous.

Amused rather than chagrined, Anthea followed him, and immediately found herself caught up in the fresh fever of Press Day.

"Does the strain never relax?" she found time to ask Odette, in the intervals of making-up for the morning show.

"The strain? What strain?" enquired Odette. "I thought you went home soon after six last night."

"Oh, I did! But I felt a rag after the high-pressure atmosphere of the afternoon," Anthea confessed. "And now it seems to be much the same tempo this morning."

Odette laughed good-naturedly.

"I went home at two-thirty this morning," she replied carelessly. "You will get used to it, *petite*."

"But what were you doing at that hour?"

"Modelling for a big charity function which started at midnight. The fee was excellent—not to be refused," said Odette, who was, like most Frenchwomen, an admirable business woman.

"But on the very night after the opening show?"

"This was what made me 'news'," Odette explained. "They like to say that Odette, the chief mannequin of

Florian"—she had the good sense to lower her voice for this provocative phrase—"came almost straight from the opening show, etcetera, etcetera. It is good advertisement."

"I suppose it would be," Anthea agreed. "Didn't Monsieur Florian object?"

"Why should he? From the other side, it is good publicity for him," Odette pointed out.

"But wasn't he afraid you would be half dead this morning?" Anthea wanted to know.

"On the contrary, he probably never thought of that," Odette replied with a shrug. "Only if I dropped dead and diverted attention from his models would he be concerned. So long as I am half dead only and do not parade the fact he would not care."

"Oh, but"—Anthea looked doubtful at this—"he's not so heartless as that, surely. In many ways, he is very kind." She thought of his quick understanding over Michael's presence yesterday.

"In many ways he is also a monster," replied Odette without heat.

"I—is he?" Anthea was a good deal taken aback.

"Of course. But if one designs like Florian one is entitled to be," Odette declared philosophically.

For Anthea this was a novel view of one's daily life and one's employer, even allowing for a certain degree of picturesque language on Odette's part. But there was no time to pursue the matter just then. The hands of the clock were nearing eleven. Madame Moisant was entering the dressing-room with her list and her air of purpose.

The Show was about to begin once more.

To Anthea there was no Press representative in Europe—indeed, in the whole world—who could inspire her with the terrors which she had felt the previous day over the presence of two mere members of the public. In consequence, she went through the Show this time calmly, smilingly and with a good deal of natural enjoyment.

There was less applause this morning, she noticed. A much more realistic, even blasé approach to the whole thing. The Press, it appeared, either was—or wished to appear—hard-boiled, and only what might be called the "dramatic" designs which might conceivably become "news" drew their grudging applause.

Among these, however, were the ostrich frond dress and the wedding dress. In fact, when the Show was over, Anthea was called out almost immediately to be not only photographed but interviewed. And, for the first time in her life, she found that she herself was news.

Before she was delivered over to the handful of questioners, Florian himself drew her aside abruptly and said,

"Nothing about either your real identity or your love affairs, mind. It's best to keep a slight aura of mystery."

Indignantly anxious as she was to assure him that she did not indulge in love affairs in the plural, Anthea had no time to linger and explain herself—even if Florian were interested, which was doubtful. She found herself surrounded and questioned and prompted, and it was all she could do to keep to the few simple, but sufficiently dramatic, facts of the real story.

Presently Madame Moisant intervened, and then the photographers had their turn.

After that, there was no time to do more than snatch a hasty sandwich before they were once more plunged into a repetition of the Show—this time for the international buyers.

This time too the atmosphere was businesslike rather than social, but the applause was not for the dramatic news-worthy designs as during the morning. It was for the "saleable" designs.

Fascinated, Anthea discovered that she was already beginning to distinguish the subtle differences in the various phases of this world. The buyers were not interested in her as news. Only in the fact that her black suit and the green lace dress would appeal to favoured customers in any exclusive store from Rio to Stockholm.

A Swiss buyer—evidently a favourite of Madame Moisant—kept her some while after the Show was ended, and, when she finally returned to the dressing-room, she heard several of the mannequins speaking in raised tones, the clear voice of Héloïse dominating the babel with,

"But of course she did it on purpose! Monsieur Florian would never arrange such a thing. She does not mind what she does to make publicity for herself! She must have waited for him—half an hour perhaps— with the photographer ready. It is shameless, I tell you! Shameless!"

"My cue, I suppose," Anthea told herself, with more calm philosophy than she felt, and she entered the dressing-room with resolution rather than eagerness.

"What is it now, Héloïse?" she enquired, in so cool a tone that the chatter ceased abruptly. Then, as though bereft of words and letting actions speak for themselves, Héloïse silently thrust a newspaper under Anthea's nose, with an air of ineffable accusation.

Anthea, surprised, took the paper, glanced at it and gasped. For splashed across the most prominent bit of the front page was a photograph of herself and Florian side by side at the entrance to the building, and above this ran the provocative enquiry, "Who is the Mystery Girl with Florian?"

Undoubtedly it was excellent of them both. Even, she noticed with irrepressible amusement, of the coat which he had repudiated. Both were glancing over their shoulders with a faintly startled expression, and this gave them an air of not quite wishing to be seen together.

Underneath the photograph was a solid block of letterpress, from which Anthea picked out some unfortunate phrases about her being Florian's "inspiration", "the unknown who saved the Show" and so on.

She tossed the paper aside impatiently.

"I can't help it if some cheap paper chooses to make a sensational story out of it," she said. "I don't like it any more than you apparently do."

"Not like it! Can't help it!" Héloïse gave a derisive laugh. "You did not perhaps have anything to do with seeing that the photographer was there at just this most fortunate moment?"

"No, of course not."

"Nor wait for the arrival of Monsieur Florian, so that you could——"

"No, of course not," Anthea said again. "It was the merest chance that we arrived at the same time. And I am not specially pleased, I tell you, to have my photograph splashed over the front page of a newspaper with that idiotic caption over the top."

Most of the other girls in the room laughed a little unbelievingly at this. But Héloïse was past dismissing anything with a laugh.

"And *I* tell *you*," she countered mockingly, "there is someone else who will not be specially pleased. You may think you were very clever to arrange this for yourself. But wait until Monsieur Florian sees it. He also does not like perhaps to be in a newspaper under this so idiotic caption. And when he hears that you arranged it——"

"I did not arrange it," Anthea reiterated patiently.

But, before she could judge if her insistence had had any effect, the door opened once more and Odette came in, followed—Anthea saw, with a slight, uncomfortable tremor—by Florian himself.

He was giving some instructions to Odette as he came, but under cover of his final words, Anthea heard Héloïse murmur triumphantly,

"Now we shall see."

It was ridiculous to feel so apprehensive, but when she heard one of the other girls say in good-natured protest, "Oh, Héloïse, don't make trouble," she could not help

50

wondering just how Florian *would* regard the whole incident.

As he turned from Odette, Héloïse held out the paper to him with her sweetest smile.

"Have you seen this, *monsieur*? Everyone—but *everyone* is talking about it."

Florian took the proffered sheet unhurriedly, and Anthea suddenly found her heart thumping.

If only he would just laugh and toss it down contemptously! Treat the whole thing with the indifference it deserved!—But perhaps it was not a matter of indifference to a famous man to be presented to his public in that silly, slightly suggestive light.

Florian did not toss the paper away. On the contrary he examined it with such thoroughness that Anthea felt apprehensively he must be weighing the effect of every unfortunate word and phrase.

Then he looked up suddenly and said in that quiet but imperious way of his,

"Gabrielle! Where is she?"

Anthea came slowly forward.

"Have you seen this?" he enquired, tapping the photograph with his beautiful, clever fingers.

"Yes, *monsieur*." She moistened her lips nervously. "But I was not——"

"The coat photographs not badly after all, *hein*?" He went on studying the picture with interest. "If this line here were shortened—— Well"—at this point he did toss the sheet down as though it were of little importance—"in a photograph of this sort one does not see much."

Anthea controlled a great desire to laugh and laugh hysterically. But Héloïse exclaimed eagerly,

"It was not so much the photograph as the story underneath that interested people, *monsieur*."

"Is there a story?" he asked indifferently.

"But of course, *monsieur*! That is the point. All about the unknown who is such an inspiration to you.

And then your arriving together in the morning, and about Mademoiselle Gabrielle being a 'mystery girl', as one says," exclaimed Héloïse, whom Anthea could cheerfully have murdered at this moment.

But Florian remained quite unmoved by all this, without even the curiosity to pick up the paper once again and see for himself what was written there. He merely smiled at Anthea, that faintly strained and yet boyish smile, and said,

"Take no notice of Héloïse's stories, *petite*. No one will take you for my mistress in that coat."

Then he went off, leaving Anthea divided between amusement, relief and a sort of chagrin which she could not quite explain to herself. While Héloïse, her big blue eyes dark with annoyance, muttered,

"There are times when Monsieur Florian is almost stupid."

"He is not the only one," Odette observed good-humouredly. Whereat the others laughed, and, to the best of Anthea's belief, the incident was closed. For if Florian himself had not objected to the photograph, who else should?

This evening she had to work later than the regular hour of departure, but it was all so interesting and every new phase was so fresh to her that, except for the weariness of standing so much, she found this no hardship. Then, just as she was at last getting ready to leave, one of the young assistant *vendeuses* came to say that she was wanted on the telephone.

"Are you sure?" So few people knew her yet in her new identity that she felt there must have been a mistake.

The little *vendeuse*, however, was quite sure. And, suddenly remembering Roger, Anthea went to take the call, with a lightening of her heart out of all proportion to the event.

It was not Roger's voice which answered her, however. It was Michael's and what he said was,

"Is that you, Anthea?—It is?—Look here, I must

see you—urgently.''

She was astounded that she could remain cool and collected. Only yesterday she had been wildly excited at the idea that he might be waiting outside for her. But this—this had come too suddenly, without preparation or time for conjecture. The very unexpectedness of it robbed it of its emotional urge.

She heard herself say gently—almost politely,

"But, Michael, I don't think there can be anything urgent between you and me. Are you quite sure that you think it a good idea for us to meet now?"

"Of course I am. Or I shouldn't have telephoned. When can I see you? Tonight? How long do you have to stay at that—dress-house?"

"I was just leaving," she told him.

"Then will you wait ten minutes and let me fetch you?"

She didn't answer that at once. She wanted madly to see him, of course, Now that the first moment of shock was past, something of yesterday's eagerness was returning. But also—which was subtly different from yesterday—there was another impulse struggling in her against acceptance, but whether it was a sense of self-protection or just plain common sense she could not have said.

"Are you still there?" he asked urgently.

"Yes."

"Well, will you wait for me, Anthea? I won't be long, I promise you."

"Very well," she said slowly. "I'll wait."

He rang off quickly—perhaps before she could change her mind—and she was left standing there with the receiver in her hand, telling herself she was a fool, and that she should never have undertaken to wait for Michael again, however superficially it was meant.

She idled away a few minutes upstairs, then went down to the *boutique* where, through the window, she could have a view of the street outside.

Mademoiselle Armande, who was in charge of the *boutique*, gave her a friendly smile and asked how the buyers' show had gone.

"Very well, I think," Anthea said. "Though I don't really know enough to judge much yet. But Monsieur Florian seemed satisfied."

"So?" Mademoiselle Armande gave her a frankly interested glance. "Did he tell you so?"

"Dear me, no!" Anthea laughed. "He doesn't make any confidences to me. But Madame Moisant had a very satisfied air when she came out of his office just now. And he has been in a very good temper all the afternoon. Though perhaps he is usually that," she added.

This made Mademoiselle Armande laugh in her turn.

"You wait!" she said. "Monsieur Florian can say more in two quiet sentences than most men in half an hour of angry repetition."

"Then I hope he will never be angry with me," Anthea said rather soberly.

The other woman shrugged philosophically.

"If you give him no reason he will not be angry. He is logical, Monsieur Florian, I will say that for him." Then she gave Anthea that frankly interested glance once more and said casually, "It was a good photograph of you and him together this morning."

"All the same, I wish it had not been taken," retorted Anthea crisply. "Some employers would have been very much annoyed."

"And Monsieur Florian was not?"

"He didn't appear to be."

"Ah!" said Mademoiselle Armande, with the eloquence which only a Frenchwoman can put into that one syllable.

But before Anthea could ask her just what she meant by that, there was the sound of a motor horn outside and, glancing out of the window, she saw Michael draw up his car at the kerb.

"I must go! Someone is waiting for me," Anthea

exclaimed. "Good night, *mademoiselle*." And she went quickly out of the building.

Michael opened the door of the car as he saw her coming, and in some odd way she felt as though time had slipped. This should have been yesterday! She had run eagerly to meet him then—and it had been Roger instead.

This time, however, it was undoubtedly Michael, and as she slid into the seat beside him, she was reminded painfully of countless other times when he had met her, when——

But it was better not to let her mind travel along those forbidden paths. Instead, she made her voice as impersonally friendly as possible and asked,

"Where are we going, Michael? Are you just driving me home or——"

"I hoped you would have dinner with me."

But no! She was not spending half the evening with him, sharpening again the memories she was striving to make dim, learning once more every turn of phrase and gesture which had been so agonizingly dear.

"I'm afraid I can't, Michael." She said that coolly, and she offered him no further explanation. "Perhaps we could go somewhere and have coffee and a—a short talk."

"Very well. Though I don't know that a short talk is going to cover it," he replied a little drily.

"But I don't understand." She was pressing her hands together now, to keep them from trembling. "What can there be left for us to say to each other, Michael—or for you to ask me, come to that?"

"There's a damned lot, and you know it," he retorted, his voice roughened and deepened with emotion in a way that was entirely foreign to him, she knew. "And the first thing I want to ask you is—what is there between you and that Florian fellow?"

CHAPTER IV

SHE was so astonished—both at the violence of Michael's words and, presumably, the violence of the feeling which had prompted them—that for a moment she could think of no reply. Then she gathered her wits together and answered spiritedly enough.

"How dare you ask me such a question in such a tone? What should there be between Monsieur Florian and me, pray? I only met him a few days ago. I'm nothing but a mannequin with the right colouring and the right measurements, so far as he is concerned."

"Then what's all this stuff about your being his inspiration and saving his show?" Michael wanted to know, though his tone was more pacific now and he was obviously impressed by her vehemence. "And how about that appalling photograph of you slipping into some doorway together, with a backward glance?"

"Don't be so ridiculous! We happened to arrive at work at the same moment. Surely you know there are some papers that would make something questionable out of a Sunday School treat. You're not a child, to start imagining things and——"

"No child ever imagined the sort of thing that's been worrying me ever since I saw that confounded paper," Michael assured her, with an unexpected flash of grim humour. "I'm sorry, Anthea. But how—and still more why—did you ever get yourself mixed up in an outfit of this kind?"

"Don't call Florian's an 'outfit', in that condescending way," Anthea said firmly. "It happens to be one of the most famous fashion houses in Paris. In the world," she added, aware suddenly that she was filled with that "local loyalty" which had amused her in others, less than a week ago. "I'm remarkably lucky to be there, I can tell you. There are girls who would give their eye-teeth for such a chance."

"And it just fell into your lap?" Michael asked sceptically.

"It just fell into my lap."

"With no assistance from the great Florian himself?" Michael enquired ironically.

"None at all," she insisted cheerfully. "Do you want to hear the story—or do you prefer the fable of me living in gilded sin?"

Michael gave her a startled glance.

"You never talked like that in the old days," he said, and something in his bewilderment touched her suddenly and wrung her heart.

"Oh, Michael—there *are* no old days now! At least, none that we should let ourselves remember. I'm sorry if I seem brighter and harder to you now. Maybe I am. Life does that to one sometimes—especially certain aspects of it. But I'm much the same underneath. So please, don't have any wild ideas about me and Florian."

"Very well. It's sufficient, of course, if you give me such an assurance," Michael said, much more gently than he had spoken so far. "I'm sorry in my turn, if I sounded suspicious and censorious."

"'Sounded'?" thought Anthea. "You were!" But she kept that to herself and aloud she said,

"It's such an extraordinary story, I know, that it's rather difficult to credit. But, if you'd like to hear it, I'll tell you just what did happen."

And so once again, but this time over coffee and to Michael, she told the story of the transformation of Anthea Marlowe into Mademoiselle Gabrielle the mannequin.

He found it much less amusing than Roger had, but he listened with even more intense interest, and asked one or two questions that were very much to the point. At the end he said briefly,

"Does your father know?"

"Father? Oh, no, not yet. I haven't had time to write and tell him. He just thinks I'm in Paris, earning my own living as a companion or translator or something."

"But you will be telling him?"

"Yes, of course. In my next letter. But I don't write all that often, you know. He doesn't expect it."

Michael frowned.

"What do you think he'll say?"

A mischievous smile flashed across Anthea's face.

"Literally, do you mean? He'll say—'Trust a daughter of mine to land on her feet. I always knew the girl would do something original.' "

Michael gave a vexed little laugh.

"You don't think he will object?"

"I don't see why he should. And, quite frankly, I shouldn't take any notice if he did. I have independence and a job which I love already. Why should he—why should anyone—object?"

Michael moved uneasily.

"It isn't the job that every man would choose for his —his womenfolk," he said at last. "Of course I believe you when you say there is—I mean, that the whole thing is nothing but a business arrangement. But frankly, Anthea, I'd rather you were doing almost anything else."

"You'd be surprised how few other things offered," she told him drily. "I was down to my last fifty francs when this happened. Madame Moisant seemed to me like an angel from heaven, and she can't have seemed that way to many people in her life."

"Anthea!" He was aghast, quite refusing to take this disclosure in the light manner she made it. "You mean that you were actually short of money? Desperately short, that is? But, my dear girl, why did you let it get as far as that? Why didn't you go home? Your father may be casual and irresponsible, but at least there would always be a home for you in his house."

58

"With Millicent?" Anthea said gently. "No, Michael, I think not. I much prefer any sort of independence in Paris to that."

He bit his lip. Perhaps he saw for the first time just what his defection had meant, in practical terms.

"I forgot Millicent," he admitted.

"Well, everything has worked out wonderfully, as it happens," she insisted smilingly. "You really don't need to worry about me."

"I shall worry, just the same," he said, and frowned as though she were still very much his concern. "I hate the thought of you in that place, with that fellow around."

"Do you mean Monsieur Florian?" she asked with rather obvious self-control.

"Of course."

"You don't really know a thing about him, do you?" she said sweetly.

"Well, come to that, do you?" he retorted.

She did not, of course, and so she remained silent. And, after a moment, Michael said stiffly,

"He hasn't the best of reputations, you know. That's why that confounded newspaper photograph was so unfortunate. Some people will think almost anything from that."

"It seems you were among them, Michael," she pointed out rather drily. "But"—she smiled suddenly in amused recollection—"Monsieur Florian himself said that no one would take me for his mistress in this coat."

"Is *that* his style of conversation to you?" exclaimed Michael disgustedly. "Very reassuring, I must say."

"Oh, dear, he was not in the least serious!" protested Anthea, wishing she had not put Michael's sense of humour to that test. "If you could only realize how impersonally he regards me, or a photograph of me, come to that. All he was concerned about was the idea that someone might thank he had designed a mass-produced coat."

Michael was rather gloomily silent, but she thought he

59

was a trifle reassured by this last statement.

"I must go, Michael." She took her mirror out of her handbag and dusted powder on her nose as though she were a busy girl with lots of engagements to attend to. "It's very kind of you to have been concerned about me, but you're worrying yourself unnecessarily. Please believe me."

He shrugged slightly.

"If you say so, that's all right."

He insisted on taking her home. And though she would have preferred him not to know where she was living, it was difficult to insist on a refusal without ungraciousness or a suggestion of pique—both of which she was anxious to avoid.

They said good-bye briefly, when the time came—a little self-consciously, because there was the shadow of too many other good-byes of a very different character between them. And, as she climbed the stairs to her attic room, she thought,

"It was a mistake to go with him. There is no such thing as two people remaining good friends when they have been in love. They must be strangers or else hurt each other all the time."

For a day or two her encounter with Michael weighed heavily on her spirits. But the demands—and, to tell the truth, the attractions—of her new life left little time for introspective thought. Like everyone else in the place—from Madame Moisant to the most junior sewing-girl, running around humbly with pins and threads—she found she identified herself with the fortunes of the House of Florian. Sometimes it astounded her, and sometimes it almost frightened her, to think that the whole of this immense organization—the livelihood of close on four hundred people—stemmed from the single brain of one man.

No wonder Odette had said, in her own picturesque phraseology, that he was entitled to be "a monster" at times.

Anthea saw little of this side of him, however, in those early days. There would be a sharp outburst of nervous anger about some trifle occasionally but, considering the strain of these fiercely competitive weeks, she supposed one could not really expect less.

To her surprise and gratification, she had not been long at the salon before she experienced her first outside success. She was asked to act as photographic model for a feature in one of the more exclusive magazines dealing with furs. And, with Florian's not altogether willing permission, she posed in mink and ermine and a fabulous silver fox evening cape which made her feel like a duchess.

"I can't wait for the article to appear," she told Roger, over another of those unsentimental but extraordinarily enjoyable little dinners. "I never expected to see myself in glossy print. And wearing about two thousand pounds' worth of furs too!"

Roger looked amused.

"Did Florian mind your doing it?" he wanted to know.

"He wasn't entirely pleased, I think."

"No? I do see his quandary, of course," Roger said with enjoyment. "He's torn between the desire to keep you exclusive and the itch to build you up as quickly as possible into a recognizable public figure, which will enhance your value."

"Do you seriously see that happening?" Anthea asked soberly.

"Of course. And sooner than you think, probably. I daresay that will be the point when Florian will try to get your exclusive services. In fact, it certainly will. He'll try to tell you that you owe everything to him, and play on your generosity that way."

"But I do owe everything to him."

"Nonsense! Only the initial chance," Roger declared with a laugh. "Give him the credit for that, if you like. But the charm and the talent and the beauty are your own. Don't you be afraid to set a high value on yourself if he does make a bid for your exclusive services. Florian's no amateur at driving a bargain! If he makes such an offer it will mean you've reached the stage of finding that people nudge each other when you come into a restaurant or a theatre and whisper, 'There goes Gabrielle.' "

Anthea laughed unbelievingly and shook her head.

"Which reminds me," Roger went on, "that you really ought to be seen at one or two big functions. It makes people notice and talk."

"Who's building me up now?" Anthea asked amusedly. "You or Florian?"

"I'm merely supplementing in a friendly way what I don't doubt Florian will do in the way of business," Roger declared with a grin. "Will you let me take you to the Charity Ball at the Crillon next Wednesday? I've forgotten what it's in aid of, but something very worthy, I'm sure."

"No, of course not. These big charity affairs cost a mint of money."

"Are you telling me I can't afford the luxury of entertaining the fabulous Mademoiselle Gabrielle?" he enquired, still with that boyish grin.

"Don't be an idiot, Roger! It's just that you've done so much for me already. I don't want to seem——"

"Two perfectly ordinary dinners and the offer of a small loan, which you refused," he reminded her scornfully. "Look, Anthea, I very much want to go to this affair. There will be several people there I ought to meet. I can't go on my own, and—to put it on the lowest plane—you're far the most attractive and presentable girl I know for a partner on such an occasion."

She bit her lip and laughed.

"You're making all this up, of course," she told him. Then she mentally reviewed her wardrobe, which showed that she was weakening.

"I haven't really anything suitable to wear for such an

occasion," she murmured, more critically clothes-conscious now than ever in her life before. "Unless——"

"Of course you have," he declared confidently, adding, manlike, "You look lovely in anything."

"That's no girl's favourite compliment," Anthea assured him absently, while she wondered if she could freshen up her ivory chiffon and make it do for the occasion.

"Please say 'yes', Anthea. It would be a real moralebooster, so far as I'm concerned."

He said that lightly enough, but suddenly she remembered that other girl who had crushed him with a much more disastrous refusal, and it seemed proportionately important that she should say "yes" at this moment.

So she said it, and told him smilingly how much she really wanted to go to the ball.

"Good!" He was openly delighted. "I'll get the tickets tomorrow."

It was impossible not to feel happy and exhilarated over the prospect. It was so long—too long—since she had gone out light-heartedly to some really festive affair, and, now that she was mastering the routine at Florian's, she felt it was time to start building some outside life of her own.

At the salon she was beginning to feel almost completely at home. For one thing, the work was no longer full of dramatic surprises. And for another she was on excellent terms with all her colleagues.

Even Héloïse seemed to have got over her initial jealousy, while Odette treated her with the indulgence of the good-natured expert and often gave her careless but very helpful advice.

Childish in most of her reactions, Héloïse showed considerable curiosity about Roger, whom she had seen both times he had come to collect Anthea.

"He is your regular beau?" she enquired of Anthea.

"No. I don't think I'd describe him as that," Anthea

said, not at all sure what Héloïse included in the term. "We are just acquaintances. Friends, perhaps."

Héloïse stared at her with rather blank blue eyes and evidently did not follow this very well.

"He is not the marrying kind?" she suggested.

"Good heavens! I've no idea. We aren't interested in each other in that way," Anthea assured her. "Nor in the way you're thinking either," she added with some exasperation, as she saw an over-understanding look come into those blue eyes.

"So?" said Héloïse, once more at a loss.

"We've really only gone out to dinner once or twice with each other. We have mutual friends in London," Anthea said, stretching the truth a little to make the position clear.

"Perhaps you go dancing together?" suggested Héloïse, who evidently found the picture so far very uninspiring.

"I'm going to the Charity Ball with him on Wednesday," Anthea conceded.

"Ah!" Héloïse was on more familiar ground. "This will be a very fine affair. Odette also is going."

"Is she?" Anthea was interested. Then she said reflectively, "I wonder what she is wearing?" and wished that her own dress had not seen quite so much service before.

"Florian is dressing her."

"*Is* he?"

"But of course. He would not wish his principal mannequin"—even Héloïse conceded Odette this on occasion—"to look anything but a credit to him. Sometimes, even, he lets one of us borrow a dress for a special occasion."

"Does he?" Anthea said. But it did not occur to her to apply this to herself. She was too much of a newcomer, she thought, for such a privilege.

So she bought a not too wildly expensive shoulder spray for her white chiffon and hoped for the best.

On the Wednesday morning, however, when she gave her dress a final inspection before departing to work, she felt anything but satisfied with it. Perhaps the weeks at Florian's had made her over-critical. Perhaps the occasions when the dress had been a radiant success were all too tarnished and dim in her present recollection. Whatever the reason, she looked at her dress with great disfavour and told herself that she would not do Roger much credit.

Now she was sorry that she had let him talk her into going. From gossip heard in the salon, she realized that it was to be a very big affair indeed—and he had been so kind to her in every way—and seemed quite proud at the thought of taking her. It was almost like letting him down.

But there was nothing she could do about it.

Work was unexpectedly heavy that day. Not only were there the regular morning and afternoon shows, but Anthea was kept very busy showing designs for a pretty South American girl who was choosing her trousseau without, apparently, needing to give even a passing thought to the ultimate cost.

Back in the dressing-room, Anthea found that most of the others had already gone and she realized that it was much later than she had thought. Only Héloïse, idling away half an hour before going to a "date", was applying lacquer to her toe-nails with the concentration of a master-craftsman.

"It's a good thing the ball doesn't start until nine." Anthea ran a comb through her hair. "I'll have time to relax a little and put my feet up before I start standing on them again." And she laughed.

"What are you going to wear?" Héloïse wanted to know.

"Oh—just a white chiffon thing I have."

"For the big ball of the season!" Héloïse transferred her attention from her toes to Anthea. "Did you ask Monsieur Florian to let you have a dress?"

"No, of course not. I've not been here long enough for special privileges."

"It's not a special privilege. You should have asked him."

"Well—I didn't think of it. And it's too late now. He went almost an hour ago. He looked in to say good night to Madame Moisant when I was there."

"You ought to wear the green lace," Héloïse went on almost dreamily. And for a moment Anthea saw herself making her entry into the Crillon clad in the Florian creation of iridescent green.

"Stop it, Héloïse!" she said with an exasperated little laugh. "I can't have the dress, and that's all there is to it."

"You could ask Madame Moisant. She also can give permission," Héloïse declared.

"N-no' I don't think I'd like to."

"Then I shall!" Suddenly and dramatically Héloïse swung her beautiful feet down from the stool on which they had been resting. "I was unkind to you at first, and in this way I will make amends." She was dramatizing herself still further and evidently enjoying herself immensely. "I shall go to Madame Moisant and ask her if you can have the dress and you shall go to the ball, like Cinderella—not in rags but in a Florian model."

And, having thus reduced Anthea's white chiffon—verbally at least—to rags, she made a splendid exit, presumably in the character of Fairy Godmother.

She was gone quite a long time. But when she returned her blue eyes were full of triumph.

"Madame Moisant has said 'Yes'," she announced. "She said 'No' at first. Twice she said 'No'. But then she thought again and said you had been very good this afternoon and that, anyway, Monsieur Florian would not want his new mannequin—so talked of—to come dowdy to the ball. You are to go quickly to the workroom and tell Mademoiselle Charlotte that Madame Moisant *herself* requires the dress."

"Héloïse, are you sure?" Anthea could hardly believe such incredible good fortune. "But it's such a responsibility, such a——"

"Of course I am sure! And it is not *so* unusual," Héloïse explained. "Twice last season I was allowed to borrow."

"Really?—Oh, Héloïse, you are a dear!" exclaimed Anthea sincerely. "I should never have dared to ask myself."

Héloïse smiled, well pleased.

"Now—what do I do? I go to Mademoiselle Charlotte and tell her Madame Moisant requires the dress——"

"And you say that it is to be booked out for the night. That Madame Moisant herself will return it tomorrow. Probably, as Mademoiselle Charlotte is a suspicious cat, she will want you to sign for the dress, and you must sign the chit with your own name and add 'For Madame Moisant'. And tell her Madame will return the dress herself tomorrow morning."

"And that really is the usual procedure?" Anthea was still doubtful about the ease of it all.

"Of course." Héloïse smiled, with a touch of experienced superiority. So Anthea—her heart light and happy—did exactly as she had been told, and all went well, except that Mademoiselle Charlotte was indeed "a suspicious cat" and said that Madame Moisant should come herself if she wanted to do such a thing.

"She would have, I expect, but she has had a very tiring afternoon," Anthea explained.

"And who has not?" Mademoiselle Charlotte wanted to know. "Still"—she shrugged—"it is her own responsibility. But you must sign here for yourself and for her."

Anthea did this, and the dress was draped lightly over her arm. It was hers!—in a manner of speaking.

Back in the dressing-room, she found Héloïse still in a co-operative mood. She had obtained one of the beautiful 'regency-striped' Florian dress boxes from somewhere, and herself helped Anthea to pack the dress.

"Oh—I must go and thank Madame Moisant!" exclaimed Anthea, remorseful that she had not done this before.

But when she ran along to Madame Moisant's office the lights were out and Madame had already gone—feeling perhaps that the South American order had delayed her quite long enough.

"Never mind. I'll thank her properly in the morning," Anthea thought, and returned to the dressing-room, to find Héloïse holding the fastened dress-box, ready to waft her on her way to a wonderful evening.

"I hope you enjoy yourself," she said, smiling so brilliantly that Anthea wished she would be like this more often.

"I'm sure I shall. The dress will make all the difference," Anthea declared. And, thanking Héloïse once more, she took the box carefully and hurried downstairs —through the now deserted *boutique*, and out into the romantic, hurrying Paris streets.

Because of the lateness of the hour and the responsibility of her burden, she allowed herself a taxi home, so that when she finally arrived safely in her room, there was time to relax, as she had hoped, and then to dress at leisure in the wonderful green model.

Roger called for her in good time, and when she heard his ring at the door far below, she caught up her evening cloak over her arm, and moved carefully down the stairs and into the lift, so that when she stepped forth he should see her right away in the wonderful dress, without any of its beauty obscured.

When she reached the gloomy hall, he was waiting for her there, having appeased the concierge in the usual manner. And as she stepped out of the lift, she heard him catch his breath.

"I thought you said you had nothing suitable to wear!" He took her hand gently, as though he thought so radiant a vision might disappear at a touch.

"I hadn't really." She laughed delightedly. "But

68

Madame Moisant let me borrow this from the Collection. Wasn't it angelic of her?"

"Angelic," Roger agreed, but he was looking at Anthea as he said it.

Then he put her cloak round her and they went out to the car together.

Oh, the joy of driving through lamplit Paris on an early spring evening! The romantic glimpse of moonlight on the waters of the Seine—the subtle, indescribable atmosphere of romance everywhere. Anthea felt it touch her like a wand of magic. And when she finally entered the great ballroom with Roger, it seemed—as the ridiculous Héloïse had said—as though there were a little touch of the Cinderella story about all this.

He danced well, she found. And all the standing and the wearisome posing of the day was forgotten. Her feet felt light and gay—and so did her heart. It was the most wonderful ball she could remember!

After a while he said, "Did you get a proper meal before you came?"

"Not really—no. I was terribly late at the salon."

"Then come on now and let's find the buffet"—he swung her out of the stream of dancers. "Too many of you girls think you can live on a lettuce leaf and a lot of excitement."

She laughed, but she came with him very willingly, for it was wonderful to be looked after again.

Others seemed to have had the same idea, and the big supper-room was already crowded, but Roger found her a space near one of the windows and went in search of refreshments.

Left alone, she looked around her on the lively and brilliant scene. So many people!—and she knew none of them. And yet she did not feel lonely—not with Roger coming back at any moment. She stood on tiptoe to see if she could catch a glimpse of him. And, as she did so, the people near her parted slightly and she suddenly saw Odette—beautiful and indescribably soignée in a

69

pale gold dress Anthea had never seen before.

She saw Anthea at the same moment and smiled in a friendly way. Then suddenly her expression changed to incredulity—and finally consternation. She murmured something to the man beside her and made her way quickly to Anthea's side.

"Are you mad?" she said softly. "What are you doing, wearing that dress?"

The smile was shocked from Anthea's face, but she answered bravely enough.

"Madame Moisant said I could borrow it."

"Madame Moisant? Impossible! Why, the dress is only three weeks old," exclaimed Odette reproachfully, as though it were a baby too young to be taken from its mother. "Do you tell me that Madame Moisant— *Madame Moisant*—herself gave you permission? You must have made a mistake, *petite*. How did she say it, exactly?"

"She didn't actually speak to me myself," Anthea explained. "She sent a message by Héloïse——"

Suddenly the most appalling chill crept down Anthea's spine, and at the same moment Odette said angrily,

"She is wicked, that one! And you—you are incredibly stupid. Monsieur Florian would kill you—but *kill* you—if he knew. How could you suppose that anyone would be allowed to borrow a model in the first weeks of the season?"

"But I understood—Héloïse assured me—that he dresses you for such occasions—that even the rest of us sometimes are allowed to borrow models."

"But not from the Collection, stupid one! Not from the *new Collection*. You must go at once, and change your dress. He is probably coming here tonight. If you are very fortunate he may be late and miss you, and tomorrow I will try to help you put back the dress without being found out. But hurry, hurry!"

"Oh, Odette, thank you for the warning! I must find my partner." And, infected by Odette's near panic,

70

Anthea turned quickly and made her frightened way towards the buffet.

She would explain somehow to Roger. He would understand. Thank heaven he understood everything so well! It would spoil his evening, but he would forgive her. How could she have been so stupid?—"*Pardon, madame*"—to a large, unresisting back. "*Pardon, monsieur*"—she slipped under an arm raised in greeting to someone.

Then she saw Roger—but he was making slowly in the other direction. She changed course abruptly, and, as she did so, knocked the elbow of someone standing near her.

"Eh—eh—*scusi, signora*," said an Italian voice, and—with a chill that reached her soul—she felt some cold liquid splashing on her shoulder.

"*No!*" Anthea said almost in a whisper. "*No!*" and she stood perfectly still at last, like someone in a nightmare, watching the red stain of wine spreading down the dress she should not have borrowed.

CHAPTER V

ALL around Anthea there was the chatter and laughter of people enjoying themselves. Their world went on though hers had stopped. Near at hand, the few people aware of her predicament expressed mild sympathy at what they evidently took to be a piece of misfortune, rather than a disaster of overwhelming magnitude. Only she knew what this moment really meant.

She was alone—alone—in this appalling situation. Even dear Roger, when he found her, could not enter into the horror of her position.

She began to move slowly back to the place where Roger would expect to find her. In spite of all the strangers round her, she felt she would have cried helplessly if she had not been too frozen and numb with horror to be able to give any expression to her dismay.

Everything was over, she told herself. Her short career as a mannequin would be ended—just as Héloïse had intended. Though even she, of course, could not have foreseen this last refinement of the disaster.

And how was she to explain to Monsieur Florian what she had done? How even attempt to justify, first her taking of the dress, and then the awful thing which had happened to it while it was in her care?

Her mind simply stopped short at the idea of finding words in which to clothe the situation.

And finally—what would *he* say? In all conscience, he would be entitled to turn his cold anger on her in the manner even Odette had rather apprehensively described. It was not to be thought of! Quite seriously she contemplated putting herself in the river, rather than face that scene.

"Anthea!" Roger's relieved voice said her name

almost beside her. "I couldn't find you anywhere. I thought——"

Then he too suddenly saw what had happened.

"I say! That's a bit awkward, isn't it?" he observed, with masterly understatement.

She nodded wordlessly. And suddenly she could have cried quite easily.

He set down the refreshments he had obtained on a nearby ledge and took her hand.

"Don't cry," he said gently. "It's not all that important."

"Oh, Roger, it is!" She spoke in a strained whisper, because her full voice just refused to come. "It seems I shouldn't have borrowed the dress in any case. I've just seen Odette, and she told me so. One of the other girls misled—misinformed me. She—Odette—says Monsieur Florian would kill me if he knew."

"I'll buy the damned thing for you. Then it'll be your dress and you'll have every right to spill wine on it if you want to," Roger told her. "Only don't look like that."

"I can't help it." Her voice dropped to a husky whisper again. "And don't make mad, generous suggestions like that or I'll start crying right here in the middle of the supper-room."

"The side," he corrected. "And quite near a convenient window alcove. Forget about the dress. I'll buy it, I tell you. It's the simplest thing in the world."

"It isn't, Roger dear, though you are an angel to think of such a thing. I can't imagine what it would cost, for one thing. And, for another, that doesn't get us out of the dilemma. One doesn't buy the dress in the Collection. One has it copied. The original dress stays in the salon to be sh-shown each day."

And at the thought of the show tomorrow with no Number Forty-two available, Anthea really did let two tears slide down her cheeks.

"Darling, don't! If this Florian is such a beast, I'm

73

not going to have——"

"*Monsieur*," said a quite and familiar voice rather languidly behind Anthea, "you do me an injustice. What is the trouble?"

Anthea felt the hairs at the nape of her neck lift, and once more the sense of nightmare was so strong upon her that, though her impulse was to scream, she could not.

Then, even before Roger or she could reply, someone took hold of her from behind and she knew it was Florian's strong, beautiful fingers that held her arms—a little too tightly.

"*Mademoiselle*, you seem to have had a most unfortunate accident to—your dress."

Slowly, and in a sort of terrible fascination, she turned her head, until her frightened dark eyes looked into his cold slate-grey ones.

"Monsieur Florian——" she whispered.

"But you must not let it spoil your evening——"

"That's what I tell her," Roger put in cheerfully.

"Without justification, *monsieur*, since you are unable to remedy the matter," Florian retorted coldly. "Come," he added imperiously to Anthea. And, with one hand still too tightly on her arm, he began to propel her towards the exit.

"Just a moment!" Roger also started forward.

"You may come too if you wish, *monsieur*."

"I damn well do wish," Roger stated emphatically. While Anthea, unable to imagine what was to happen next, submitted helplessly to Florian's direction—as she would have if he had been leading her then and there to the block.

Out on the crowded landing, he spoke briefly to someone who seemed to be in authority, and they were all three bowed into a lift and wafted up a couple of floors.

Here they were conducted to a beautifully appointed bedroom, at which point Roger said,

"Just what is going on?"

"It will help, *monsieur*, if you neither question nor

comment for a few minutes," Florian told him curtly, and rang the bell for the chambermaid.

While they waited for her, he stood back from Anthea and considered her critically. She went pale under his cold, thoughtful glance, even when she realized suddenly that it was at the dress, and not herself, that he was looking.

Then he came forward and, while she gasped at the ruthlessness of it, he ripped most of the stained lace bodice from its foundation, tossing it on the floor, as though it no longer concerned him.

Roger started forward at what seemed to him an outrageous gesture towards any girl. Then, suddenly realizing what was happening, he hesitated.

Florian, taking no notice whatever, next detached— with the same bold, decisive movements—two of the beautiful floating panels from the skirt, and began calmly, and without haste, to fashion these into an exquisite draped bodice.

By the time the chambermaid entered, the whole of the upper part of the dress was transformed, and the skirt merely lacking in a little of the fabulous fullness that had distinguished it.

"Pins," he said to the woman, without even looking at her. "And a needle and thread."

She stared, open-mouthed, at what was going on. Then she gasped,

"I have only white thread, *monsieur*, for the linen."

"Very well. It will do."

She trotted off briskly and returned almost immediately with the required articles. Then she—and, to tell the truth, Roger too—watched fascinated while Florian coolly secured his matchless draping with a few quick stitches.

"There!" He stood back from Anthea once more. "It will hold for the evening, if you are not too energetic, *mademoiselle*. And you, *monsieur*," he added, with an ironical little smile, "must not embrace her too heartily, or you will probably find some of my pins."

75

"Oh, Monsieur Florian, I—I don't know how to thank you," Anthea stammered.

"You have no need to thank me, *mademoiselle*," he said icily. "It was a case of restoring my model rather than consoling my mannequin, I assure you."

Suddenly she knew what Odette had meant.

"Please, please let me explain," she began, as he turned to go. But he silenced her with a slight gesture of his hand.

"I have no time for explanations now, *mademoiselle*," he said with terrifying gentleness. "We have wasted enough of the evening as it is. But you will explain to me tomorrow morning—in full."

Then he handed the chambermaid her sewing materials, and with a slight bow to Roger, went out of the room, leaving them to follow at their own pace.

The chambermaid absently held out her hand and Roger absently put something into it. Then, taking Anthea by the arm, he gently led her out along the heavily-carpeted corridor.

"Well, it wasn't so bad, was it?" he smiled down at her.

Anthea could not answer. She wondered how he could have been so deaf to the overtones in Florian's voice. Or was it just that, in her terror, she imagined things?

"I must say he made a wonderful job of repairing the damage." There was reluctant admiration in Roger's tone that time.

"Yes," Anthea managed to say.

"Do you have to worry any more?" he smiled down at her, a little teasing, but a little coaxing too. And suddenly she remembered that this was his great evening. He had planned for it, paid heavily, she had no doubt, for it, and now she would not—*would* not spoil it for him.

Even if Florian sacked her tomorrow—which he undoubtedly would do—even if he pulverized her first with the weight of his cold anger, this was Roger's evening,

76

and she determined that he should enjoy it.

She flashed a smile up at him.

"No," she declared, "I don't have to worry any more, I—I can hardly get used to the idea! But Monsieur Florian has made the dress look wonderful again. And —and I don't even have to think about how I shall tell him what happened. He—he knows."

"Sure. And he said you could explain to him in full tomorrow. I bet that other girl will get the sack."

"Which other girl?" enquired Anthea, who could think of only one girl getting the sack.

"Why, the one who misled you into thinking it was all right to borrow the dress, of course."

"Héloïse? Oh no! No, really I can't imagine that happening to Héloïse."

"Why not, for heaven's sake? Is she his girl-friend?"

"Of course not! But Héloïse is just not the sort to get the sack," Anthea explained drily. Because she knew at last that, for all her air of big-eyed simplicity, Héloïse was simply the kind who saw to it that someone else got the sack. But never, never herself.

"Well, if you think he'll be indulgent all round, that's all right," Roger said comfortably. And Anthea forbore to say that that was not at all how she expected Monsieur Florian to be in the morning.

Much later in the evening, she encountered Odette once more. And, after staring at her inexplicable young colleague for a moment, Odette halted her very distinguished-looking partner and, with a word of excuse, came over to Anthea.

"I thought you were going home to change, Gabrielle," she said in a severe tone. Then suddenly she looked at the dress as though she thought she were losing her mind.

"What—what has happened?" she said, almost in a whisper. "It's—*different!* You have—— No, you can't have been so mad as to change a Florian model. Besides"—she put out her hand and touched the bodice

77

with experienced fingers—"only one person can drape like that."

"Why, Odette, how clever of you!" Anthea smiled feebly. "You're quite right. Monsieur Florian did it himself."

Odette swallowed.

"I don't understand," she said helplessly.

"Someone spilt wine on the dress as it was," Roger began to explain cheerfully, but Odette uttered a little cry at this and actually turned pale.

"Monsieur Florian saw," explained Anthea, continuing the story doggedly, though she thought it sounded dreadfully improbable as she told it. "And he made me come with him—and he altered the dress, as you see, in not much more than ten minutes."

"You say"—Odette looked at Anthea as though she were not quite sure whether to call her a liar to her face or salute her as one who had emerged from the jaws of death unharmed—"you say Monsieur Florian *knows* what has happened?"

"Yes, yes, Odette. It's all right, really." Anthea glanced quickly at Roger who was smiling unconcernedly at her side. "But it was all done so quickly. There will of course have to be some explanations tomorrow."

"That I can well imagine," agreed Odette feelingly.

"But tonight—I'm just enjoying myself. Monsieur Florian said I was to," she added, extending the meaning of certain phrases rather unpardonably.

"So?" said Odette, and turned away, evidently under the impression that neither truth nor sense could be expected from any prolonging of the conversation.

"She seemed to take a rather serious view of it all." Roger looked after her thoughtfully. "Look here, Anthea, if there's going to be any real trouble over this business, you'd better let me——"

"No, no, Roger! There's no need for you to get involved," exclaimed Anthea, determined not to cause him any more anxiety or trouble. "Odette is always a bit of a tragedy queen. It's part of her stock-in-trade. You don't need to worry. I expect there'll be a few sharp words over the explanations tomorrow, but nothing that could justify any intervention from outside."

"Are you sure?" He was not entirely satisfied, she could see.

"Yes, of course. Perfectly sure," she lied desperately.

He said no more just then, and she thought he was satisfied. But when, much later, he had driven her home, under a night sky that was already paling into early dawn, he stopped her, just as she would have said good night and got out of the car.

"I'll call for you tomorrow—or, rather, this evening. I want to know that you got on all right over this dress business."

"Oh, Roger!" She nearly put her head down on his shoulder and wept, but she controlled herself in time. "You—you don't really need to, you know. But—if you want to——"

"I want to," he stated pleasantly and finally.

"Then—then I won't pretend I shan't be glad to think of that when I go in to make my explanations in the morning," she admitted with a faint smile.

Then she thanked him a little huskily, said good night once more, and ran into the house, hoping he would take her haste for anxiety over the lateness of the hour and not the need to struggle again with tears that were near the surface.

Trembling with fatigue, she carefully took off the green lace dress, trying conscientiously not to disturb the lightly secured work which Florian had done actually on her. She wondered what he would do about the dress now. Would he let it be worn as it was until a duplicate of the original model could be made, or would he withdraw it altogether from the Collection for a while?

It was a purely academic query, she assured herself, because *she* would not be wearing it in any form. Not after what had happened this evening.

Tired though she was, she could not sleep even when she was in bed. She lay there, watching the pale square of her window and wondering what was to become of her.

It was the "lowest" of all the twenty-four hours, and Anthea saw herself once more penniless and workless in Paris. But, strangely enough, even this vision did not wring her heart so truly as the thought that Florian's would know her no more.

She knew now—amazedly—that she had come to love the place with something like passion. Not only for the glamour—of which there was very much less than most outsiders supposed—but because of the wonderful, thrilling sense of excitement and achievement. For good or ill, for now and always, she felt, she was part of Florian's. Even when she was dismissed and cast off with contumely, she would still feel miserably that she was part of Florian's. But for ever exiled and repudiated.

Anthea sobbed a little to herself at last. Then she slept fitfully. But only fitfully, since she must not add to her terrible list of offences the final one of being late that morning.

When she woke, it was with a sense of disaster that set her heart thumping, and made her throat feel dry. But, since she was essentially courageous, she got up, dressed with meticulous neatness, and drank some hot coffee, though she could not face the thought of food.

Then, carrying the beautiful striped box, which contained the evidence of her crime, she set out for Florian's —possibly, she supposed, for the last time.

It required all the courage she had to enter the familiar portals and mount the long staircase to the dressing-room. She felt as though everyone who saw her and called out a greeting must wonder why she was carrying a dress-box, and suspect what it contained.

And then, of course, the next thing was to get rid of it. There was no one else yet in the dressing-room. But she could no more leave one of the models lying about (even in its mutilated form) than she could leave a corpse unconcealed. The two things seemed rather similar in Anthea's mind at the moment.

So, finally, she went boldly upstairs to Mademoiselle Charlotte, still carrying the box.

"I've brought back Number Forty-two, *mademoiselle*," she said timidly.

"Where?" enquired Mademoiselle Charlotte briefly.

"Here—in this box."

"In a *box*! Madame Moisant had no right to put it in a box," declared the angry Mademoiselle Charlotte, who carried on a long series of skirmishes about such matters with the *Directrice*, in order to prove her own importance.

Anthea then remembered that Madame Moisant was supposed to have borrowed the dress, and she saw further and agitating complications ahead.

Desperately she cut at least this Gordian knot.

"Mademoiselle Charlotte," she said, as calmly as she could, "there was some misunderstanding about this, which I can't explain in detail. But Madame Moisant did not borrow this dress. I did."

"*You* did!" Mademoiselle Charlotte looked almost as though smoke might come out of the top of her head. "*You* borrowed a model from the NEW COLLECTION— for your own use? You stand there and tell me—quite calmly—that you practised a wicked trick on me and borrowed a dress from the Collection? You, who have not been here a month!"

All the time she was speaking, she was ripping the cord from the box, raising the lid, casting aside clouds of tissue paper and, finally, lifting out the dress. At this point she uttered a loud scream.

"It is not the right model!" she exclaimed, her voice running up the scale and cracking with emotion. "It has been changed."

"I know," Anthea said wearily. "Monsieur Florian changed it himself last night when——"

"Monsier Florian—last night?" Mademoiselle Charlotte's tone changed subtly to a note of astonishment, mingled with the caution of one who was not going to put her foot in it, however improbable the circumstances. "What—what were you and Monsieur Florian doing last night, pray?"

The highly questionable wording and the sudden change of manner made Anthea want to laugh hysterically.

"We were both at the Charity Ball—but separately," she said curtly. "Someone spilt wine on my dress——"

"*Your* dress!" Mademoiselle Charlotte seemed ready to laugh hysterically in her turn.

"All right—this dress. Monsieur Florian saw what had happened and changed the dress into what you see now."

"Right there in the ballroom?" The Frenchwoman sounded incredulous, but as though all things were, of course, possible to Florian.

"Certainly not! In a private room on——"

"A private room, eh?" Madame Charlotte smiled sourly.

"My partner was there too," Anthea explained patiently, wondering what other misunderstandings and innuendoes she was going to have to struggle against. "As a matter of fact——"

"I do not understand what you are talking about," exclaimed Mademoiselle Charlotte, suddenly rejecting the whole story. "And, moreover, I do not believe a word you are saying."

"Well, I can't help that," Anthea retorted, with a little spurt of nervous temper. And she went downstairs once more, leaving Mademoiselle Charlotte to make what she liked of the whole affair.

Several of the other girls had now arrived, and among them Héloïse. She looked fresh and smiling and was humming a tune to herself, as though she were without a care in the world or a shadow on her conscience.

"Héloïse"—Anthea went over to her and spoke

calmly and almost politely—"why did you pretend to me last night that Madame Moisant had given permission for me to borrow the green lace dress?"

Héloïse stopped humming and turned astonished blue eyes on Anthea.

"Madame Moisant?—green lace dress?—I don't know what you are talking about," she said blandly.

Anthea gasped. In all her experience so far she had never met the cool, confident and out-and-out liar.

"Héloïse," she said, and her voice shook a little, "you know perfectly well that you sat in here last night, painting your toe-nails and telling me that we were sometimes allowed to borrow models. And you said you would ask Madame Moisant if I could borrow——"

"*I* would ask Madame Moisant if *you* could borrow?" Héloïse laughed scornfully. "Why should I? I do not like you," she stated, simply and with devastating truth this time. "Why should I do this for you?"

"You mean you deny the whole thing?" Anthea's voice was suddenly grim as she realized what she was up against.

"I do not deny anything. I simply say you are telling silly lies which I do not understand," Héloïse assured her pleasantly. And, still humming to herself, she turned back to the mirror and began to make up skilfully.

Anthea stood there for a moment, silent and still. She should, she supposed, have been ready for something like this. Obviously Héloïse would have had no intention of allowing her real guilt to be pinned upon her. But this! —This absolutely blank denial of everything was shattering in its completeness.

She glanced round for Odette, who might at least say something in support of her. But Odette had not yet arrived—and, in any case, could not substantiate Anthea's story further than to say that, when seen in the dress, she had spoken of Héloïse's assurance that she might borrow it.

The situation could hardly have been worse. But,

whatever one's personal misery, the work of the day had begun. Anthea too took her seat before the mirror, and absently passed a comb through her hair. As she did so, she saw in the reflection of the glass that the door had opened and Madame Moisant had come into the room.

She bit her lip. First with nervousness, and then with the sudden idea that she just might possibly enlist Madame Moisant's aid.

It was a forlorn hope, really, born of desperation. But the fact was that the *Directrice* was not so wildly unreasonable as some of the people round her. Besides, she had been responsible for bringing Anthea here and, in that sense, regarded her in something of the light of a protégée.

If she could be made to believe the truth——

Anthea turned impulsively towards her. But as she did so, the door opened again, and one of the secretaries put in her head and said,

"Mademoiselle Gabrielle in Monsieur Florian's office, please!"

CHAPTER VI

THE blow had fallen!

Somehow, Anthea had not expected it quite so soon. Monsieur Florian usually did not put in an appearance until rather later in the morning, and she had imagined herself with another hour of grace—or dreadful anticipation—as one cared to look at it.

But, in spite of his late night, he had evidently made a point of arriving early. And it seemed that her melancholy affairs took precedence over everything else.

"Hurry!" Madame Moisant said, as Anthea seemed for a moment unable to move. "One does not keep Monsieur Florian waiting."

There was the faintest edge to her voice and Anthea saw she was not too pleased. She preferred any contact between Florian and the mannequins to be made through herself.

In spite of Madame Moisant's admonition to hurry, Anthea went up to Héloïse and said quietly,

"I warn you that I shall not attempt to shield you. I can only hope to clear myself if I tell Monsieur Florian exactly what happened."

Héloïse merely glanced at her and shrugged, as though to say she neither followed, nor wished to follow, what Anthea was talking about. It was so perfectly done, and left such an impression of blank ignorance, that, as she went from the room, Anthea thought, with a sense of added chill,

"If it comes to her word against mine, who would believe that she is lying?"

Monsieur Florian's office was on the next floor, and Anthea found she was completely breathless when she reached the top of the stairs. Not because of the steepness of the ascent, but because her frightened breathing had become a series of short, shallow gasps.

She stood for a moment outside his door, resisting the terrible panic-stricken impulse to turn and run from the place. Then, calling on all her powers of resolution, she knocked.

"Come in!"

He spoke in English, showing that he guessed who was there, and, with a confused sort of prayer in her heart, Anthea opened the door and went in.

Florian was sitting at a big, highly polished desk, which gave him an air of formality and remoteness that was unfamiliar. As she entered, he picked up the telephone, asked the switchboard girl for a number, and silently indicated a chair to Anthea while he waited for his connection.

Then, with a refinement of cruelty which made her remember what Odette had said of him, he conducted a conversation of several minutes with one of the big silk manufacturers, exactly as though the unhappy girl before him were not there.

By the time he replaced the receiver, Anthea felt sick with suspense.

He made a note on a pad beside him, then he looked up and fixed his cold, unsmiling grey eyes upon her.

"Now, *mademoiselle*"—his voice was unhurried and pitched on its usual quiet note—"perhaps you will tell me how you came to be wearing a model from the Collection at the ball last night."

"I thought I had Madame Moisant's permission," she said huskily.

"You thought? It is as well to be sure on these matters. But if Madame Moisant is to be brought into this, she had better be present to hear what is said." And he stretched out his hand towards the bell on his desk.

"No, no! Please don't send for her!" cried Anthea, feeling that Monsieur Florian was enough to cope with at the moment, and so urgently did she speak that he drew back his hand. "May I—may I just explain in my own words first?"

"That, *mademoiselle*, is what I have asked you to do," Florian said drily.

"But—without any sarcastic interruptions," she begged him with the boldness of desperation. "And in —in some detail."

He looked at her with very slightly narrowed eyes for a moment, as though to decide whether or not she were trying to trick him. Then he made a gesture with his hand, which she took to be permission to speak on.

She must be absolutely calm and circumstantial, she told herself. This was her one chance. And, moistening her lips nervously with the tip of her tongue, she launched into the story.

"Monsieur Florian"—she gripped her hands tightly together in her lap to keep them from trembling—"when I was asked to go to this ball, my first impulse was to refuse, because I had nothing really suitable to wear. But the friend who invited me wished very much to have me with him, and as I owed him very much kindness, I decided to make do with a—a not very new, but reasonably presentable white chiffon which I had.

"I can't say that I was happy about the dress, *monsieur*, particularly"—she smiled palely—"after what I had learned here in the last few weeks. But I never thought of anything else, right up to last evening, when I was preparing to go. It was late and only—only one other of the girls was left in the dressing-room.

"She knew I was going to the ball—they all knew— and she asked what I was wearing. When I told her she seemed horrified and said—why had I not asked you to lend me a dress?"

Florian's eyebrows went up but, true to her request for no sarcastic interruptions presumably, he said nothing.

"I told her I had no idea that such a thing was even possible and that it was, in any case, too late now. She seemed very anxious to help and declared that, since you

87

were gone, she would go and ask Madame Moisant herself. She went——"

"To Madame Moisant?" He did interrupt that time.

"I had no reason to think anything else then, *monsieur*."

"Very well. Go on."

"She came back, saying that Madame had given permission—that I was to fetch the—the green lace dress from Mademoiselle Charlotte, and sign for it in my own name, but on behalf of Madame Moisant."

"And you believed all this nonsense? You must be simple indeed, *mademoiselle*," he exclaimed impatiently.

"Why should I *dis*believe it, *monsieur?*" retorted Anthea. "You forget that a month ago the dress world was a closed book to me. It was only when Odette saw me at the Ball, and expressed her horror, that I understood: How should I know what the conditions were in so special a case? What do you know, for instance, of the procedure followed when someone working at—at" —she thought fleetingly and nostalgically of Roger— "one of the Foreign Embassies has to take home a 'top secret' document for further study?"

There was a slight silence. Then over Florian's clever, rather worn face there flitted the characteristically boyish smile.

"Frankly, nothing, *mademoiselle*," he conceded with unexpected candour.

"You—you see?" She was startled herself by the success of her simile. "I was in a similar position."

"And greatly tempted," he added a little mockingly. "Because you wanted to look beautiful for the erring lover who had returned to you."

"I wasn't even tempted," Anthea insisted. "Because I didn't know that what I was doing was wrong. And as for wanting to look beautiful for—— For *whom*, did you say?" Suddenly his exact words penetrated her consciousness.

Monsieur Florian did not reply at once. He hardly seemed to notice the note of denial in her tone.

"*Mon enfant*," he said at last, and the unexpectedly gentle term of address brought a sudden lump into Anthea's dry throat, "when I first saw you in my more or less ruined dress, I assure you my first impulse was to strangle you. Certainly I wished to humiliate you and dismiss you in front of everyone. Then I saw the big, hulking Englishman who was consoling you by calling me names, and it became suddenly clear to me that you had—unpardonably but understandably—borrowed the dress, in some way not clear to me, in order to impress this man who had left you for someone else."

"But I assure you——" began Anthea.

He silenced her with a peremptory but not unkindly gesture.

"I am not a sympathetic man by nature," Florian said drily, "but I suppose we all have moments when we see with sudden clarity into soneone else's feelings. Angry though I was with you, I *could not* humiliate you in front of him. Nor did I wish to bring your evening to an abrupt and disastrous end so early. There was only one thing to do"—he shrugged—"repair the damage as well as possible and postpone both explanations and censure until the morning. But that did not really lessen my anger with you."

"No, *monsieur*," she said softly.

"And now you tell me that, foolish though you have been"—he looked at her penetratingly—"someone else is more to blame. Which of the other girls gave you this—bad advice?"

She had felt so angry with Héloïse earlier that morning that she had thought she would not care at all about giving her away. Now, in spite of everything, she found the name stuck in her throat.

"Monsieur Florian, I would rather not give the name," she said hesitatingly. "In any case, she denies the whole thing completely this morning."

He made a sound of nervous exasperation. Then suddenly, as though some inescapable instinct stirred within him, he glanced at his watch.

"Quick!" he said sharply. "The morning show is about to begin. If you hurry, you will be just ready for your first entry. I will deal with this other matter later."

Obedient to the note of urgency in his voice, Anthea sprang to her feet.

"But, Monsieur Florian, won't you even tell me——"

"I will tell you nothing," he cut in shortly. "You will not tell me who this offender is. Very good. I also can play that game. Now go."

She went. There was nothing else to do—particularly with the time of the morning show so near. But at least he had not dismissed her! At least he had not crushed her with the full weight of his cold anger.

Back in the dressing-room, with Madame Moisant scolding, and the other girls exclaiming at her lateness, Anthea had no time for anything but to slip into her black suit and make ready for as cool an entry as she could achieve.

It was incredible how irresistibly the show went on, however distracted one was feeling. Anthea found herself sauntering up and down the long platform, smiling, twirling, going through all the usual motions. It seemed that nothing could interfere with the usual march of events.

Almost nothing. When the show had been in progress ten minutes, a note was brought to Madame Moisant and, glancing at it with a gasp of surprise, she turned to Anthea and said,

"Number Forty-two will not be shown this morning. I have a note here about it from Monsieur Florian."

"Very well, *madame*," Anthea murmured meekly.

"What happened?" Odette found time to whisper. "Have you seen Monsieur Florian?"

"Yes."

"And is he—letting you stay on?"

90

"I don't know. We hadn't quite finished—finished discussing it all when it was time for the show."

"O-oh!" Odette's sceptical tone indicated that she found it hard to believe that anything had been dealt with at discussion level. And she gave a rather discouraging shake of her head before going out to show the black velvet ball gown which made her look like something out of the third act of *Traviata*.

It was over at last. Even the breathtaking wedding gown had been shown once more, to the sound of a chorus of murmured approval. Nowadays, with the earlier excitement muted to more everyday routine, there was seldom applause, but there was no lack of admiration, shown in quieter ways.

Anthea returned to the dressing-room for the last time, and had just changed from the wedding dress when Monsieur Florian entered with an air of cold purpose which set her heart fluttering again.

"Madame Moisant, I wish to speak to all the girls." He ran an eye over them to see that they were all present. "I shall be obliged if you will also remain."

Madame Moisant, who was intensely curious about everything that went on at Florian's, would not have left for worlds. But she inclined her head graciously, to indicate that she remained at Monsieur Florian's express wish.

He turned back to the mannequins who had instinctively clustered together near the long mirror, and again his glance travelled over them, but more slowly this time.

"An unfortunate breach of rules occurred last night," he said, in that quiet, arresting voice of his. "One of the mannequins borrowed a model from the new Collection——"

"Impossible!" ejaculated Madame Moisant.

"—and wore it at the Charity Ball," finished Monsieur Florian, unmoved by the interruption.

"As you will realize," he went on, in the deathly hush which had suddenly fallen on the room, "there is only one way of dealing with such an offence, and that is—dismissal."

"Monsieur Florian," exclaimed Odette at this point, "there were extenuating circumstances in this case which I think you should——"

"Thank you, *mademoiselle*, I am aware of them. You have no need to assist me in this matter."

Odette subsided. But, to her credit, she took Anthea's hand, as though to say that she was with her. While Madame Moisant, suddenly remembering the note which had been brought to her, turned to look at Anthea and hiss, "Number Forty-two!" like someone in a thriller.

"I understand," Florian went on, still speaking quietly —almost conversationally, "that the girl who was foolish enough to borrow the dress did so on the earnest advice of a fellow mannequin, who, obviously, could only have done this with the idea of getting her into trouble."

For the third time, he looked over them reflectively.

"When I spoke of dismissal for the offender, there was only one girl here who did not look dismayed. Héloïse, why did you look pleased at the idea of a colleague being dismissed?"

"I, *monsieur*?" Blue-eyed astonishment was turned upon him by Héloïse. "You are mistaken."

"No, Héloïse." Monsieur Florian was superbly calm and unshaken. "I am never mistaken about my mannequins. I know you all probably better than you know yourselves. How else could I design the clothes that express you exactly? You were quite satisfied—even happy—at my announcement."

Héloïse dropped her eyes. Florian was the only one who could make her do that.

"*Monsieur*, you exaggerate," she murmured, with an air of being forced to the truth. "I was not really happy—elated—about it. But—I am frank—I do not like Gabrielle, and I was not actually sorry to hear that she would go."

"I did not speak of Gabrielle," he said coldly. "How did you know she was the one in question?"

"But—but——" Héloïse stammered. "I thought—I supposed——"

"Of course. You thought I must be speaking of Gabrielle because you had arranged for her to be trapped into borrowing the dress."

"*Monsieur*——" Héloïse began to cry. "You are unjust. I never intended——"

"That will do, Héloïse. This is not a good moment for tears," Florian said drily. "In the circumstances, Gabrielle will not, of course, be dismissed. And—count yourself lucky in this—you too will have only a reprimand and a warning. But it is a serious warning. I should not be prepared to overlook such a thing again. Remember that, and do not overestimate yourself not underestimate me. You are stupid, Héloïse," he went on almost carelessly, "and without conscience, but because you have a great deal of sex appeal you find a place in my salon. Do not, however, make the mistake of thinking you are indispensable. To be indispensable one must either be clever and without conscience or perhaps a little stupid but with an exact conscience."

Then he turned to Madame Moisant.

"*Madame*, Number Forty-two will be replaced as soon as possible. Until then we shall have to omit it from the Collection."

"But—I don't understand!" Madame Moisant shot a disapproving glance at Anthea, who was standing, pale and wordless throughout all this, unable to take in the fact that Florian himself had cleared her. "Has Number Forty-two been *lost*?"

"No. It met with—an accident." Florian smiled faintly. "It was necessary to change it at a moment's notice. In its present form it is not what I want for the Collection. An entirely new one will be made."

"And—the other one? The one which was, as you say, changed at a moment's notice? Where is that?"

"Where is it, Gabrielle?" Florian turned suddenly to Anthea.

"I—I took it back to Mademoiselle Charlotte this morning."

"I see."

"Part of it can be used, surely?" Madame Moisant said.

"I think not." Florian's glance rested thoughtfully on Anthea. "It was altered specially to suit Gabrielle. I think perhaps, in the circumstances, we should let her have the dress."

"A Florian model—as a gift!—after doing anything so silly and wrong?" Madame Moisant was scandalized. While Anthea could only stare at Florian with suddenly enormous dark eyes.

"*Monsieur*," she said, almost in a whisper, at last, "I have done nothing whatever to deserve it. Very much the reverse, as Madame Moisant says. To be—given—a Florian model!"

"Somewhat altered," amended the great designer exactly. "You have had a bad twenty-four hours, *petite*. I do not see why you should not now have a little pleasure out of the incident. Particularly as—or perhaps in spite of the fact that—you refused to give Héloïse away and put me to the trouble of finding out for myself who was responsible." He patted her cheek rather sharply, which brought a little colour into it to relieve the pallor.

"Monsieur Florian, I don't know how to thank you!"

"By wearing the green dress, of course, and never again resorting to the not very new, but reasonably presentable white chiffon," he replied a little mockingly.

Then, turning to Madame Moisant, he asked her about the big South American order, and almost immediately they went out together, talking of business affairs.

The moment they had gone, the other girls crowded round Anthea—with the single exception of Héloïse, who retired to sulk in a corner, though not with any real sense of shame or depression. For, though Florian had called her both stupid and conscienceless, he had also said she had considerable sex appeal, and no insult to her intelligence or disposition could take precedence with Héloïse over the fact that even Florian had had to admit the gift which had been bestowed upon her so lavishly.

"Well! It is all very happily ended." Odette, who was usually singularly unemotional, actually kissed Anthea. "I could not have believed it would be so."

"Nor could I, Odette! I'm so—so relieved, I could cry," Anthea declared. "It's like waking up from a nightmare."

"To wake up with a Florian model is not bad," remarked one of the other girls mischievously.

"She will not be satisfied with the model for long," put in Héloïse viciously. "Next it will be with Florian himself."

This fine disregard for the law of slander drew cries of laughter and protest from the girls, but Anthea was not unaware of the fact that one or two of them glanced at her curiously.

The rest of the day was extraordinarily uneventful— almost an anti-climax to the drama of the morning— but late in the afternoon Madame Moisant sent for Anthea.

She glanced not unkindly at the rather exhausted-looking girl who came in.

"You will do well to go to bed early tonight," she remarked. "Late nights are evidently not for you."

Anthea forbore to say that the shortness of the night had been the least of her stresses and strains during the last twenty-four hours.

"Yes, *madame*," she said submissively.

"Sit down, *petite*."

Anthea sat down.

"Now—it is not for me to censure where Monsieur Florian has been indulgent," Madame Moisant said impressively. "But I must warn you that never again must you suppose that I would *send* a message of importance. Invariably I *give* such a message in person."

"Yes, *madame*. I realize that I should have thought of that," Anthea admitted remorsefully. "I did come along to your room to thank you before I went, but you had already left."

"No doubt." The other woman's tone was dry. "Héloïse would have made sure of that before she started this escapade. You should have known better than to trust her after the jealousy she had shown in the beginning."

"But she had been so friendly lately, *madame!* I just thought she had got over her jealousy and was rather sorry for what she had done."

"Jealousy is one of the few emotions one does not get over," stated Madame Moisant profoundly. "And the Héloïses of this world are never sorry for what they have done. Only sometimes—a little—for what they have not done. I am afraid you are a little naïve, *mon enfant*, and that is not good in this particular world."

"I'll remember," Anthea said soberly. "I'll be careful about Héloïse in future."

"Oh—Héloïse!" Madame Moisant laughed slightingly. "There will be no more trouble with her. What I wished to say is that you should be careful with *all* the people around you. You must not think so easily that because a person is kind—or generous"—Madame Moisant moved a few articles unnecessarily on her desk —"that person is a friend. I give you this warning because you are a good girl and I would not wish you to be made unhappy."

"Thank you, *madame*." Anthea was touched and faintly puzzled, but she acknowledged the kind feeling behind all this with her sweetest smile.

"*Bon!*" exclaimed Madame Moisant with an air of satisfaction. "Then we understand each other, *hein*?"

"I am sure we do," Anthea agreed, still smiling.

Madame Moisant smiled graciously, and indicated that

Anthea was now free to go.

It was nearly six o'clock, and she remembered with a delighted skip of her heart that Roger would be waiting for her—under the impression that she would come forth crushed and miserable.

Well, it would be fun to tell him all about it. It was fun to tell Roger anything. He found her so amusing and interesting that he always put her in a good frame of mind with herself. Than which there is no pleasanter feeling.

Anthea had always wished to have a brother. Now, with Roger in the background, it was almost as though she had. Almost.

He was waiting for her in the car, as usual, when she came out, and greeted her with an air of careless good humour which did not altogether hide a certain amount of anxiety.

"Well," he asked, almost before she had taken her seat beside him, "how did it go! You look very cheerful, so I take it you were not actually given the sack."

"Given the sack? I was given the frock," retorted Anthea, laughing immoderately in her delighted relief and amusement. "Oh, Roger, what a day! Do you want to hear all about it?"

"Why do you suppose I'm here?" he enquired, with an amused glance at her. "Go ahead. I was prepared to console you if necessary, but I'm just as pleased to stand on the sideline and cheer the victor."

She laughed again, and for a moment put her hand over his on the wheel.

"Roger, you're not like anyone else! Don't think I ever take you for granted, will you?"

"You can take me as you like, so long as you take me," he retorted lightly. And at the moment it did not strike her that this was not a particularly brotherly way of putting things.

Instead, she began to give him an account of the morning's dramatic happenings—right down to the point where Florian decreed that the dress was to be hers. By the time she had finished the story they had reached their favourite little restaurant on the other bank of the river. Then, as they leaned their arms on the check-clothed table between them and drank red wine while they waited for their meal, Anthea added an amusing account of her interview with Madame Moisant.

"So she thinks you're a lamb among the wolves, does she?" Roger gave her an amused, indulgent glance.

"Apparently," said Anthea, breaking off pieces of crusty bread and eating them with enjoyment. "I don't know quite why she thought it necessary to warn me so particularly, since she seems to think there'll be no more trouble with Héloïse. But it was nice of her to bother."

"Very nice," agreed Roger reflectively.

"She said, at the end, that no doubt we understood each other now."

"And did you?" enquired Roger, again with that look of indulgent amusement.

"I *said* I did," Anthea admitted with a smile, "but I don't know really what she was talking about—except in a general way. But then I suppose she meant it only generally, don't you?"

"No. I suppose," Roger said slowly and in his most matter-of-fact way, "that, very tactfully and obliquely, she was warning you against Florian."

CHAPTER VII

"AGAINST Florian?" Anthea looked extremely startled. "But why should Madame Moisant want to warn me against Florian, for heaven's sake? He couldn't have been kinder or more understanding over this ghastly business."

Roger was silent. And, after a moment, Anthea asked hesitatingly,

"Do you—do you think she had *reason* to issue some warning against him?"

"I don't know, my dear." Roger shrugged, still with that good-humoured air of not taking any of this very seriously. "I don't know him. Dress designers are not exactly up my street. But he didn't strike me last night as the sort of chap who went about giving away models, out of the goodness of his heart."

"Didn't he?" She smiled faintly. "That's just how he does strike me."

"Dear girl! It's unusual in the dress trade. Or any other trade, come to that."

"But then Florian is an unusual person. I don't mean that he's crazily generous. I think he is often hard and a little cruel, and almost always a very good business man. But he has a romantic streak. Almost all great artists have—and he is that. I can imagine that he might, on a sudden generous impulse, quite enjoy giving away one of his models—out of the goodness of his heart and nothing else at all."

"Well—it's a nice theory," Roger conceded, with a grin, as their meal was set before them.

"Roger, you're not being very serious about this, are you?"

"Is it a very serious matter?"

99

"Well—yes. I think it is."

"But my dear, if you are forewarned—and you have been by both Madame Moisant and myself—I can't think that you're in very great danger."

"Me?—in danger? I wasn't thinking of me," Anthea stated rather indignantly. "I was thinking of Florian—and not wanting to do him an injustice.—Oh, no, it's not even that! I don't *want* to have to find him an amorous schemer, who only gave me that dress because he thought it was a good move. I want to think of him as the great man with a romantic flash of generosity who——"

"Yes, I do see what Madame Moisant means," Roger said, handing her the salt. "Go on with your dinner, my little sheep among the wolves. Your Florian is a great artist, as you say. He is also a very good business man, as you say. The two together can produce some very fine and very reprehensible things. But most of all they will produce some unpredictable things. That being so, it is best for you not to suppose that you can interpret his actions in romantic terms. He may be one of the wolves—I don't know. But one thing is certain," Roger finished with a grin. "Florian is not to be counted among the sheep."

Anthea smiled reluctantly.

"I suppose you're right. But this is the last moment I should be prepared to think badly of him."

"Hence Madame Moisant's very timely warning," declared Roger. But he did not pursue the matter beyond that point, and Anthea could not help thinking how pleasant it was to have him keep everything on an amusing and good-humoured level. Michael would have made terribly heavy weather of this interview.

And, thinking of Michael in this mood, she suddenly found she could speak of him quite naturally, where previously she could not have brought herself to ask even the simplest question about him.

"Roger, did Michael and Eve stay on in Paris? I've

never—asked you about them."

"And I've never told you about them, because I didn't know if talking of them would hurt."

"It's all right—now."

"Is it, my dear?" He glanced at her with that quizzical but curiously reassuring smile. "Well, they stayed about a week after you saw them at the opening of the Collection. Then they both went back to London. But"—he hesitated a moment—"I had a letter from my aunt this morning—Eve's mother, you know—and she said Eve was returning at the beginning of next week, for dress fittings or something of the sort."

"I see. Will she be—coming to Florian's?"

"I couldn't tell you. She went around to most of the dress shows, but what arrangements she made I just don't know, Anthea."

"It doesn't matter," Anthea said quickly. But of course it did.

"I'll have to act as escort to her during the time she is here," Roger said rather stolidly. "I'm the only member of the family here, and my ties with that branch of the family used to be strong when we were all much younger. My aunt would think it odd if——"

"Roger dear, are you thinking it necessary to make excuses to me?" Anthea smiled at him. "It isn't in the least! Of course you must take your cousin around. Why ever not?"

"It seems disloyal," he said quite simply. And suddenly she could have hugged him for such uncomplicated thinking so unashamedly expressed.

"It isn't disloyal," she said gently. "But thank you for thinking that way. Will she be here long?"

"Some days, I suppose. Perhaps a week."

"Then during that time please feel that she has first call on your time, and if we don't manage to get together I shall quite understand."

"We shall manage to get together," he assured her, and she felt a warm sensation of contentment steal over her.

The next day she awaited her summons to Florian with considerable interest. But when she was finally sent for, late in the afternoon, he had little to say to her, and that little was said in Mademoiselle Charlotte's presence, since that lady attended in person to see what was to be done later in her workroom.

Anthea had rather supposed that she would find an opportunity to tell him of his mistake about Roger and Michael. But any private conversation was impossible with Mademoiselle Charlotte's bright, beady eyes upon them and her thin ears almost quivering with the desire to hear something scandalous, or at least enjoyably questionable.

He might have been working on a stuffed dummy for all he noticed the girl who was eventually to own this wonderful creation, and for Mademoiselle Charlotte it must have been a disappointing session.

Curiously enough—so contrary is human nature—it was faintly disappointing to Anthea too, though why she could not have said.

Roger was out of Paris for the weekend and Anthea spent a delightful, lazy Saturday on her own. Sitting at the open window of her attic room, with the soft spring air of Paris stirring her hair and caressing her cheek, she wrote a long letter to her father, telling him in a lively, carefree way about her life at Florian's.

"It's to be hoped Millicent won't think from this that I can get Florian to dress her free," Anthea thought with grim amusement. But Millicent—and even her father—seemed faintly unreal people at this moment. Only Paris and Roger and the life at Florian's seemed intensely real.

Possibly because writing to her father had put her in the mood for it, on Sunday she looked up some friends from the old days who had a country villa just outside Paris.

They were delighted when she telephoned, and insisted on her coming out there to lunch.

"It's such ages since we've heard anything of you, darling," declared Laura, the second girl in the family, who had answered the telephone. "What are you doing these days?"

"I'm modelling at Florian's."

"You're *what*?"

"Modelling at Florian's," repeated Anthea, aware of an intense pride and delight in her job.

"But, my dear, how thrilling! Do you mean you wear glamorous clothes all day long?—and see famous customers? And is he as fascinating as people always say he is?"

Anthea laughed.

"I do wear glamorous clothes, but not all day long, and all the customers aren't famous. And I don't know how fascinating people say Florian is," she answered precisely.

"Don't be so aggravating!" was the delighted reply. "Just come out right away, and be prepared to tell us everything. Florian! Imagine! He's one of the three men I've always wanted to meet, the other two being Laurence Olivier and the Duke of Edinburgh. Now hurry."

So, amused and not unflattered by the sensation her announcement had caused, Anthea made her way out of Paris to the country, which was just beginning to break out into the first beauty of spring.

She was received affectionately and with intense curiosity, not only by Laura Daviot and her family, but by the one or two guests who had also dropped in. Everyone wanted to hear what it was like to work at Florian's, what was *really* the new line for the season, and, above all, what she knew of the famous designer himself.

"I've heard he is always courteous, even when he's being perfectly beastly," Laura said, rolling her fine eyes upwards. "Is that true, Anthea?"

"He practically never raises his voice, if that's what

you mean," Anthea replied carefully.

"Even when he's being beastly?" Laura insisted.

Anthea thought of him sitting at his desk telephoning, while she waited in anguish for him to deal with her. But then she also thought of him patting her cheek sharply and saying that the green lace dress should be hers.

"I don't think he's ever beastly," she said loyally, if not quite truthfully.

"There you are, you see! She's fascinated by him," declared Laura mischievously. "They say people always are. She can't see a fault in him."

"I didn't say that," Anthea retorted. "But he's a good and very just employer."

"Oh, my dear, how dull! You only have to add that he is industrious and honest and you've destroyed the whole Florian illusion!"

"He's not dull," Anthea stated positively.

"I should think not, indeed." That was one of the visitors, a sophisticated-looking girl who had not joined in the general laughter over Laura's nonsense. "Is it true that he had a long affair with Peroni, the opera singer?"

"I haven't the least idea," Anthea said, immediately acquiring an unreasonable distaste for this questioner. "I'm not in his private confidence."

"But there must be heaps of gossip about the place," Laura protested. "Surely you'd hear something. Do you have to be so discreet?"

"I heard nothing about Florian and any opera singer at any time," Anthea insisted drily.

"Well, it might have been before you went there," the other girl said carelessly. "He's supposed to have someone else now, isn't he? Some mystery girl or other. There was a photograph of them going in somewhere together, with a very surreptitious air, about a month ago. They said she was his new inspiration or something."

Anthea felt herself flushing, but whether with anger

104

or embarrassment she was not quite sure.

"That was no mystery girl. That was myself," she said curtly. "And I never inspired him to anything yet."

Everyone laughed, and Laura asked, with obviously uncontrollable curiosity,

"But where *were* you going, together?"

"Into the salon, of course. Don't be silly," retorted Anthea. "I suppose the other stories about him have just about as much foundation in fact."

"Oh, I shouldn't think so," the sophisticated-looking girl insisted, and Anthea actually found herself wishing she had not come.

Florian's private life had nothing whatever to do with her, of course. She was not even called upon to defend him, just because he was her employer. But—although it had been fun at first telling them about her life and making them all amused and curious—now, she found, she wanted to change the subject.

With some difficulty, she contrived to do this. And—though she hardly admitted to herself that the move was dictated by any feeling of unease—early in the afternoon she insisted that she had to go back to Paris.

"Not anything to do with your work on Sunday, surely?" Laura said.

"In this case, no," Anthea agreed. "Though some of the girls do photographic modelling then. At the height of the Season there's little other time."

"It all sounds rather like penal servitude in mink, to me," Laura declared. "But I suppose the life has great compensations."

Anthea supposed so too. But she was not sure that she and Laura were thinking of the same compensations.

Back in Paris, she felt her spirits revive and her heart begin to rejoice. Even with most of the shops shut, and the weekday bustle and vivacity muted, how beautiful the place was! And, in some small way, Anthea thought, she belonged to it all.

This was her bit of Paris. Here she belonged.

The news that Eve Armoor would be returning to Paris had given Anthea an unpleasant jolt when Roger first told her, but she had thrust it resolutely to the back of her mind. She was therefore singularly unprepared when, two days later, Madame Moisant sent for her to display the wedding dress to a customer and, on coming into the mirrored fitting-room, she found that the customer was Eve.

"Hello, Anthea." Eve smiled at her brittlely. "Miss Marlowe and I have known each other a long time," she explained aside to Madame Moisant.

"Miss Marlowe?" Madame Moisant looked as though she considered any Miss Marlowe an entirely hypothetical person. "Ah, you mean Mademoiselle Gabrielle. Is that so?"

"Oh—you're Mademoiselle Gabrielle here, are you? How quaint," Eve said, with a laugh. Then, practically ignoring Anthea, she turned once more to the *Directrice*.

"I loved this dress when I saw it at the Opening," she explained. "But my fiancé was not so keen as I. However, I feel that Monsieur Florian is definitely the man I want to design my wedding dress. I thought if he——"

"Shall I see if Monsieur Florian is available, *madame*?" Madame Moisant said, and sent a junior *vendeuse* running to find the great man himself.

Anthea stood there rather still, trying to look exactly as she would look if any other customer were discussing wedding dresses. If she could manage not to show any of the reactions which Eve wanted her to show, then the victory was hers. But it was so hard that she knew every muscle and nerve was tensed.

Then Florian came in, and in some unaccountable way Anthea felt the tension relax slightly.

He was charming to Eve, but shook his head immediately when she began to explain how much she had liked the wedding dress when she saw it on the opening day.

"It is not for you, *madame*," he said. "It does not

106

express you in the least."

"No—that's what my fiancé said," declared Eve with a laugh, while Anthea felt morally certain that Michael had never used such a term in his life. "He thought it looked wonderful on Anthea—on Gabrielle—— We both know her, you know," she explained in smiling, condescending parenthesis, "but for me he thought more—more——" She waited for Florian to fill in the gap.

Instead, he looked reflectively at her.

"More what, *madame*?" he said at last.

"Oh—I don't know——" Eve laughed, faintly put out, though it obviously puzzled her to find that she was. "What would *you* suggest?"

He sat down, without answering her, and began to sketch rapidly. Madame Moisant took up her polite conversation again, though in slightly more subdued tones, and Anthea went on standing there. Until actually dismissed, she could not go.

"Only until the end of the week this time," she heard Eve say, in answer to Madame Moisant's enquiry about her length of stay. "There's a gala performance at the Opéra on Friday and I want to go." For a moment her glance went, faintly maliciously, to Anthea. "Roger is taking me—Gabrielle. I wonder if you would like to come too?" she said.

Astonishment at such calculated spite—without, after all, much reason—robbed Anthea for a moment of the power to reply. Then, without even looking up from his sketching block, Florian said, in that quiet, almost conversational tone of his,

"Unfortunately, Mademoiselle Gabrielle is already committed to going with me."

Eve gasped slightly. So did Madame Moisant, but she managed to turn it into a suppressed sneeze.

"To—to the Gala at the Opéra?" Eve said.

"To the Gala at the Opéra, *madame*. Now—if you will look at this. I would suggest—— Oh, you need not wait, Gabrielle," he said, with a slight smile at Anthea.

And Anthea slipped away, not quite sure what had happened, or why this extraordinary proposition had been made. That Florian's few quiet words had rescued her successfully from Eve's malice was obvious. But that he should have known what was going on—and, still more, that he should have acted on that knowledge, bewildered her.

She saw no more of Eve, she took part as usual in the afternoon dress show—and she waited to see if either Florian or Madame Moisant would send for her to give her any further information about this sudden—or perhaps purely illusory—visit to the Opéra.

It was Florian who sent for her, towards the end of the afternoon.

This time he was not sitting in state behind his desk. He was walking about the room, in that slightly restless way which was characteristic of him and, as she came in, he paused to light a cigarette.

"Come in, Gabrielle," he said, seeing her hesitate in the doorway. "We must discuss the question of the Opera Gala."

She came in.

"Monsieur Florian, I did not know——"

"No, of course you didn't," he interrupted impatiently. "I didn't know myself until this afternoon. But it is not unusual for me to use an occasion like this to display some very particular model. Odette is usually chosen, because everyone knows she is my chief mannequin. But this time I wish to use you. And, as you are not yet known as part of my salon—at least, not generally so—it is necessary that I should accompany you. Otherwise——"

"Monsieur, why are you doing this for me?" Gabrielle asked quietly. "You knew, of course, that Miss Armoor was the girl who took away the man I was to marry. You realized—though I cannot imagine how—that she was there this afternoon to humiliate me, quite as much

108

as to choose her wedding dress. Good—it is very kind of you to feel sympathy for me. But why go out of your way to help me?"

"*Mademoiselle*, you flatter yourself." Monsieur Florian smiled slightly. "I intend to show a particular model on that night, and I wish you to wear it."

"But *what* model, *monsieur*? Even you cannot create *and have made* a completely new dress by Friday. This is already Tuesday evening."

"I don't propose to create a new dress. You will wear the one I am giving you."

"Oh, Monsieur Florian! It is the most wonderful dress in the world to me, but you can't make me believe that you would arrange a special gala visit to the Opéra to display a—a modified version of Number Forty-two in the present Collection," Anthea exclaimed. "Even I am not so new and simple as to think that."

He actually laughed slightly—a rare thing with him.

"You are indeed new and simple, *mon enfant*. Over the dress you will wear an evening cloak which will make Paris gasp. That is what you will be displaying at the Opéra. It did not need to be made on you. It is almost ready. You will try it on tomorrow and then it will be completed. I take it you are free—or can make yourself free—to come with me to the Opéra on Friday."

"Of—of course," stammered Anthea.

For a moment she accepted his explanation so completely at its face value that she thought she really had been mistaken in supposing that the visit had been arranged for her benefit.

But then she remembered the quiet, unexpected words which had so completely disconcerted Eve.

"Monsieur Florian, you explain very plausibly." She smiled fleetingly at him. "But I find the whole thing too *à propos* to believe that it was not partly designed to save me from further humiliation at Eve Armoor's hands."

109

He smiled and shrugged, as though to say that he would not argue further if she insisted on her own story.

"Tell me," she said curiously, "how did you—how did you guess what she was getting at?"

For a moment she thought he was still going to disclaim all knowledge of what she meant. Then he smiled slightly and said,

"I remembered that the big Englishman, who so charmingly called me a beast, was also addressed by you as 'Roger'. When she suggested that you should make a party à trois, it was not difficult to see that one should—prevent that. But prevent it with the explanation that you already had a more distinguished escort," said Florian without any false modesty.

"Oh—oh, I see!" She laughed a little doubtfully. "I'm afraid I have never been able to explain to you that —that Roger is not really the man who turned me down. He——"

Up went Florian's very clear-cut eyebrows.

"You mean this is a second admirer whom she also wishes to acquire from you? But, *mademoiselle*, this is too much! Why did you have to let her know that this one also admired you?"

"He happens to be her cousin, Monsieur Florian—and she knew him many years before I did," Anthea confessed with a smile. "I don't know that he does 'admire' me particularly, come to that. We're just very good friends."

Monsieur Florian muttered something about the British being incomprehensible.

"I'm so sorry!" Anthea looked at him and laughed with real merriment. "It was still a most welcome rescue, I assure you. If my heart was not greatly concerned, my pride undoubtedly was. I *hated* her at that moment, and had no defence at all. When I heard you say I was to come to the Opéra with you I—I could have——" She remembered suddenly that she was speaking to a distinguished Frenchman, not an easy-going and understanding Englishman, like Roger, for instance. So she coughed slightly and left her sentence unfinished.

Florian, however, missed little.

"What could you have done, *mademoiselle*?" he enquired with real interest. And his second use of "*mademoiselle*" instead of "Gabrielle" showed her that he was regarding her at this moment as a woman instead of a mannequin.

"Oh—I—don't know," she said quickly, and blushed. "Anyway, I can't thank you enough. But—you don't really have to make good the invitation, if you would prefer—I mean, you have no real *reason* for taking me, now that I've explained about Roger and—and Michael."

At the introduction of Michael's name he looked a little as though he thought the explanations had been rather incomplete even now. But he said, with that faint, charming smile which was usually kept for most favoured clients,

"I was going to the Opéra on Friday night, in any case, and no man asks for a reason for taking a beautiful girl with him on such an occasion. It so happens, *mon enfant*, that it—suits me very well to have you there then. In the cloak I have designed."

"Well then, there is nothing more for me to say except —'Thank you very much,'" Anthea told him. And she thought that his little nod of dismissal had indulgence as well as amusement in it.

That evening, instead of going straight home, she walked down the Champs-Élysées, looking for one of those huge circular street stands on which all the many amusements and attractions of Paris are dis-played. If she was going to the Opéra with Florian on Friday, it might be as well to know what she was to hear.

She found what she wanted at last—not in the detailed,

smaller printed announcement that covered the opera
dates for the week, but splashed in large capitals across
a big yellow poster on its own—

Vendredi—2 *avril: TOSCA.*

Then, in only slightly smaller print underneath—
Floria Tosca—Giulietta Peroni.

"I see. Then you won't need me as chauffeur." He paused. "Is Nicole not to expect Fifine back then, either, then?

CHAPTER VIII

ANTHEA read the announcement of the gala performance at the Opéra twice. Then she turned away and walked on rather soberly down the Avenue in the fading spring twilight.

Peroni. She remembered the name perfectly well. That not very likeable girl at the Daviots' had spoken of her and had declared there was supposed to be—or to have been—an affair between her and Florian.

There was no need to take that very seriously, of course. More than likely it was some absurd rumour. For, thought Anthea shrewdly, the girl was the kind to spread innuendoes and half-truths. But if she had been right——

Anthea found that she disliked the whole idea quite passionately. Once more she assured herself that Florian's private life was no concern of hers. If he cared to go to the Opéra to hear an old flame—or even a present flame—of his, who was she to have views one way or the other about it? Even if he took her too.

For her part, she would be attending simply as one of Florian's mannequins, displaying a creation of his. Incidentally, thanks to some sort of kind impulse on his part, she would also have the very welcome opportunity of cutting a good figure before Eve, who had wished to humiliate her.

There was really nothing to worry about. If only he had not said—"It so happens, *mon enfant*, that it suits me very well to have you there."

Why did it suit him very well to have her there?

At the time she had given him the credit for wishing to put her at her ease, by implying that it was she who was doing him a service, rather than the other way round. But now she was not so sure.

113

She knew it was foolish of her to seek so earnestly for motives and to split hairs over something which she was never, in any case, likely to know much about. But—it was just as she had said to Roger when Florian gave her the green dress—she *wanted* to see him as the great man who made a generous gesture. Not as someone who used her just a little for his own ends.

Curious how often he made these seemingly generous gestures. And afterwards one wondered if there had not perhaps been some ulterior motive behind them.

She was a trifle shocked to discover this, and thought remorsefully that perhaps the fault was in herself rather then Florian. She even wondered if her experience with Michael had made her sceptical and unable to believe in generosity for its own sake. And, in case this were the fact—and she was doing less than justice to the man to whom she owed so much—she determinedly dismissed the whole thing from her mind.

But it returned, of course. Particularly when, the next day, she caught a glimpse of Florian, and he gave her that brief, faintly enigmatic smile and said, as he passed,

"The dress is completed, I hear. We will try it—with the cloak—this afternoon after the show."

"Very well. Thank you, *monsieur*," she said composedly, and went on into the dressing-room where, most unusually, she found Odette sitting alone—her feet up on a chair, in the automatic attitude which all mannequins assume in moments of rest.

"Odette"—Anthea spoke on sudden impulse—"I'm to go to the gala performance at the Opéra with Monsieur Florian on Friday, and wear some wonderful cloak he has just designed."

"So?" Odette glanced at her quite benevolently. "I heard it was probably to be you. Mostly he uses me for these occasions, but it seems the cloak is too—soft and young and 'endearing' was I think the word Monsieur Florian used. For me the designs must be dramatic."

"Oh," Anthea said rather thoughtfully. "What sort

114

of cloak is it, do you know?"

"White mink," Odette told her carelessly.

"White mink!—I should have thought that was dramatic enough," Anthea exclaimed, at which Odette laughed.

"It depends on its use," she said.

"I—suppose so."

There was a slight silence, while Odette went on reading a fashion paper and Anthea considered the use of the word "endearing".

Then Anthea spoke again, rather determinedly.

"Odette—do you often go out with Monsieur Florian to display designs in this rather—rather more subtle way?"

"No. More often I go alone or with an escort of my own choosing. But then everyone knows I am his mannequin, and so they know also that any model I am wearing must be one of his. With you it is different. Until he has made you famous—and I think perhaps he wishes to do just that—it is necessary that he accompanies you."

"Yes—I see. He said something of the sort himself."

"You need not look so solemn, *chérie*. You will enjoy yourself. Monsieur Florian is a charming escort. And it is always pleasant to be looked at very much in our profession," Odette said.

"Of course," Anthea agreed hastily. "But—Odette, have you ever been to the Opéra with him?"

Odette slightly wrinkled her beautiful forehead and obviously made an obliging effort to remember.

"Once—yes. About three years ago, when I also was not so well known. I recall it was the *première* of some modern opera. Inexpressibly boring," Odette said reflectively. "But I contrived to look interested throughout the evening, since we were sitting in a *loge* and very much on view," she added, with a touch of professional pride. "Afterwards I found this was quite unnecessary since all the critics had been bored too and said so the next day."

Anthea laughed.

"Who sang, Odette?" she enquired carelessly.

"How do you mean—who sang?"

"Who was in the cast?"

"*Petite!* How should I know at this date?" cried Odette, to whom the opera had evidently been of less than no importance. "I remember nothing at all except the dress I wore and the terrible length of the time between the intervals, when of course I strolled about with Monsieur Florian and was, most discreetly, on show."

"I see." Anthea bit her lip, and then, seeing that the indirect method was getting her nowhere, she asked outright. "Did you ever hear Peroni? She is going to sing on Friday night. In *Tosca*."

"*Tosca?*" Odette smiled approvingly. "Ah, there is an opera in which something happens! All die—and violently. You will enjoy yourself."

"I'm sure I shall." Anthea agreed hastily, wishing that Odette had not taken up the wrong part of her remarks. "But did you ever hear Peroni?"

Odette, who had rare but keen flashes of humour, looked amused then.

"Never. Nor do I know if she is really Florian's '*amie*'," she said. "Which is, of course, what all this conversation has been leading to."

Anthea flushed and gave a rather vexed little laugh.

"It's not just curiosity——"

"No?" said Odette, to whom curiosity was a perfectly natural and commendable trait which required no excusing. "What then?"

"Oh—never mind. But, tell me, Odette. You know him so well that——"

"Florian? No one knows him well," Odette interrupted. "He is the complete enigma. It is part of his stock-in-trade."

"Is it?" Anthea was startled. "Well, then—in your experience, let us say, is he what you would call a generous person?"

116

"Financially—no. But it is difficult to be a successful business man and financially generous," Odette admitted tolerantly. "If, however, you mean—is he capable of sudden flashes of imaginative generosity? I think—yes. Just as he is capable of sudden cruelty," she added thoughtfully.

"Like the time he gave me the green dress?" Anthea said, ignoring the remark about cruelty.

"It could be." Odette measured her with a considering glance. "I could not say. It was also, of course, a little bit of posing."

"Posing, Odette!"

"Of course. Either to you or himself," Odette replied indulgently. "Like most great artists he is something of a *poseur*. And why not? The great should be allowed their foibles. Only the foibles of the mediocre are insufferable."

"Bravo, Odette!" said Monsieur Florian, coming in at that moment. "Of whose foibles are we speaking?"

Anthea was struck dumb with confusion, but not so Odette. She had been longest with Florian and was least afraid of him. Besides, as she never presumed on her position in minor matters, she even occasionally allowed herself the indulgence of speaking frankly to him.

"Yours, *monsieur*," she said, with her slow smile. "I was telling Gabrielle that you are something of a *poseur*."

"A *poseur*?—Am I, Odette?"

To Anthea's amazement, he sat down on the side of the long dressing-table with—for the first time in her experience of him—an air of relaxing for a few minutes. And he smiled consideringly at his chief mannequin.

"At times, *monsieur*. But aren't we all in this profession?"

"I suppose we are, Odette. Except Gabrielle." He suddenly included Anthea in the conversation with that curiously boyish smile.

"I, *monsieur*?" Anthea opened her eyes rather wide. "Why should I be an exception?"

117

"Because you don't really belong to this world, of course. That is why you wear all the subtly unsophisticated models well. And the wedding dress. Gradually you will change"—he gave her a half amused, half discontented look—"and then I shall no longer design wedding dresses for you in the soft, cloudy materials. It will have to be satins and taffetas and tissues. Possibly even velvet——" Both his tone and his glance were changing, as though, in his mind's eye, he already saw a slightly older, more sophisticated Anthea before him.

"And suppose I do not change, *monsieur?*" Anthea spoke softly, but, in some odd way, challengingly.

"You are bound to, *petite.* That is what life does to us," Florian told her drily.

"Some sort of change—yes. But not necessarily such a change as you suggest. One can also, I suppose, become warmer and richer in personality, instead of colder and—more arid."

"But one cannot remain unknowing." He still spoke half smilingly, but with an undercurrent of something like bitterness. "It is because you are so—so unknowing that you can look at the world so wide-eyed—and be taken in by the Héloïses and the—what was it?— the Michaels. And wear my wedding dress the way you do," he finished with a short laugh.

"You make me sound very simple," Anthea protested, not too pleased.

"Eh, *mon dieu*, why not?" exclaimed Florian impatiently. "What do you suppose is the rarest thing in the whole of this shattered, cynical, unbelieving world of today? Simplicity, of course. Simplicity in its basic, classic, lost sense. You have it, *mon enfant.* That is the whole basis of your appeal. Though it might be better for yourself if you were capable of a few suspicions," he added, with a sort of half-cynical regret.

Anthea was silent for a moment. Then some mischievous, daring impulse which she could not possibly

118

explain to herself prompted her to say,

"So you think I am incapable of suspicion, Monsieur?"

"Almost entirely." Florian's cool, quick glance had already gone to the wrist-watch that ruled his life at the salon, and he moved to stand up again.

"You make me ashamed, *monsieur*," Anthea said softly. "For I actually entertained some suspicions towards you."

"Towards me?" Half startled, half amused, he looked at her again, his attention wholly recaptured. "In what way, *petite?*"

"It was very ungenerous of me." She bent her head, so that her fair hair fell forward, shadowing her face a little. "When you gave me the green dress, I was at first so happy. I thought only a great man would be so generous in those circumstances. And then—I am sorry now—I wondered if *even* a great man might have some ulterior motive."

There was the oddest silence. Then Florian said abruptly,

"Look up. And stop play-acting."

She looked up immediately, a good deal startled by the fact that he saw through her so easily.

"You did not think of that on your own," he told her. "Only—someone put the idea into your head, and you thought this would be an amusing way of finding out the truth."

"Oh, Monsieur Florian——" She was a good deal ashamed of herself by now.

"I gave you the dress, *mon enfant*, because I wished to give you pleasure," he stated slowly and categorically. "There was no ulterior motive——"

"Oh, Monsieur Florian!" she said again remorsefully.

"—though I suppose there might well have been," he added with characteristic realism

"*Sans doute*," put in Odette with equal realism.

But Anthea was not for realism at the moment. She

was overwhelmed to think that she had met generosity with suspicion. Still more that she should have made her suspicions a basis for some rather unworthy play-acting, as he had called it.

"This time I am truly ashamed," she said and, coming over, she took both Monsieur Florian's hands in hers, which seemed to surprise him not a little. "Please forgive me. You're quite right. It wasn't my impulse to distrust your wonderful gift. But afterwards I was not proof against the suggestion. I feel very mean about it —and would like to thank you all over again for your—your goodness to me over the whole incident."

"You have a very charming way of making amends, *petite*, for suspicions which you had every right to entertain," Florian said. Then he glanced down at the hands which still held his and, raising them, kissed them very lightly, one after the other, before firmly withdrawing his own fingers,

"Odette"—he turned to the other girl—"I need you in my work-room in ten minutes."

"Yes, *monsieur*," Odette said, and looked thoughtfully after him as he went out of the room. Then, as the door closed behind him, she remarked to Anthea, "Four years and two months I have worked for Florian, and I have never seen him do that before."

"Do what?"

"Kiss the hand of a mannequin."

"O-oh. Well, it was a rather special occasion."

"Was it?" Odette said, and swung her feet to the floor. "And yet you never voiced your real suspicions to him. So that you are completely in the dark still about them."

"What do you mean?" Anthea came and sat beside Odette, who was beginning to apply her very light make-up.

"You never really thought Florian used the dress as a first bait to lure you into a naughty situation," Odette said, smiling at Anthea in the glass with an air of friendly

120

scorn. "That was someone else's idea, as he said, and you just toyed with it a little. What you really want to know is—Does he take you to the Opéra on Friday night for your pleasure, or for purposes of publicity, or merely to make Peroni think that he has a younger and prettier and more *piquante* girl to play off against her?"

Anthea was silent for a moment. Then she said,

"I couldn't ask him any *more*."

"No, of course not. Do you think he didn't know that too?"

"Oh! Do you mean he deliberately lulled any suspicions I might have in the future by making me ashamed of those I hadn't really had anyway?"

"I don't know." Odette laughed exasperatedly. "I tell you—no one every really knows what Florian is thinking. You can suspect him of the darkest designs, if you want to. Or you can set him up in your mind as the most romantic and generous of creatures. The one theory is as likely to be right as the other. I must go now."

And, with a final touch of colour on her lips, she got up from the long dressing-bench and went off, leaving Anthea once more in a mood of sober reflection.

Before she could get very far, however, someone looked in to say that she was wanted on the telephone. And, with the delighted certainty that it must be Roger calling her, she jumped up and hurried to the telephone.

It seemed a long time—really, much too long—since she had heard his pleasant, matter-of-fact tones, and she felt her spirits rocket as he said,

"Hello there! Have you got any time to spare on a minor diplomat this evening?"

"Oh, Roger, I'd love to."

"I've parked—my family responsibilities with some-one else this evening, and though I'm working late and can't actually fetch you from Florian's, I thought we might have a bite together and perhaps do a late film, if you would like that."

121

"Of course I should. Shall we meet at our usual place?"

"If that's all right for you. Eight o'clock."

"Eight o'clock."

"Here, what's this about your going to the Opéra with Florian?" Roger enquired, just as she was about to ring off.

"Nothing—really. I'm just going to show off a model of his. Besides—— Oh, well, I'll tell you all about it when we meet."

He laughed and agreed to this. Then he did ring off, and Anthea went off to the routine business of the day.

In the late afternoon she was summoned to Monsieur Florian's work-room. And here, under the eagle eye of Mademoiselle Charlotte, the green lace dress had its final fitting.

Then the cloak was brought. And Anthea, who had awaited this moment with the liveliest curiosity, found she could not even cry out at the sight of it. Her ridiculous, inexplicable reaction was that she felt a lump in her throat.

Here Florian had used the most luxurious, the most queenly, the most opulent of furs for a design of such exquisite and deceptive simplicity that one could think only of the purity of untouched snow or the innocence of childhood.

"Monsieur, every woman in the Opéra will long for it," Anthea said, almost in a whisper.

"Few, however, will be able to afford it," commented Mademoiselle Charlotte with a grim chuckle.

"Few, also, would be able to wear it," Florian said, as the cloak was put round Anthea's shoulders, and she slightly inclined her cheek to the exquisite caress of the collar.

"Nonsense. It will go to some knowledgeable harpy with a rich boy-friend," Mademoiselle Charlotte declared, with no belief in the rightness of things.

"Then it will look quite a different thing, of course,"

122

Monsieur Florian said calmly.

"Oh, but what a shame!" Anthea exclaimed. "It's like—like cruelty to children. Couldn't you refuse to sell, if it was for someone perfectly horrid?"

"I could, *mademoiselle*. But I should not be the successful man I am if I did business on those lines," Florian assured her with a smile. While Mademoiselle Charlotte cackled derisively at the idea.

"There is no sentiment in business," she told Anthea, and gave her a slight push, as though she were a child who had said embarrassingly silly things in company.

"But on Friday night it will look as it should," Florian said, surveying Anthea from all angles. "That should do."

She was not quite sure if he meant that the model was satisfactory or that even a white mink cloak must be satisfied with one crowded hour of glorious life. But she smiled at him over her shoulder and knew suddenly that she was going to enjoy Friday night.

That evening, when she met Roger, there seemed to be such a lot to tell him. And yet it was not quite a week since she had seen him.

Already, of course, he knew something of Eve's visit to the salon—though only her side of it. And Anthea filled in the details, and explained about Florian's sudden intervention with the statement that she was accompanying him to the Opéra.

"And was that the first you'd heard of it?"

"Of course."

"His rather eccentric way of letting you know the great man had decided?" suggested Roger, frowning as though he were not altogether pleased over the idea.

"Oh, no! He thought Eve was 'needling' me—which, of course, she was—by telling me she was going with you, and suggesting I should trail along as an unwanted third. But Florian thought it was even worse, because he had an idea that you were Michael," Anthea explained not very lucidly.

"*What?*" For the first time in her knowledge of him,

Anthea saw Roger really annoyed.

"Oh, Roger—it's all rather confusing——"

"It must be."

"I hope you're not really mad about it, but, you see, right away in the beginning—on the day of the Opening—I told Florian that the man who'd turned me down was there in the salon——"

"Good lord! Was that necessary?"

"Oh, it just came out. The way these things do sometimes when you're excited or under a great strain. Then something I said later made him think Michael—the man concerned—had some doubts about his second choice and——"

"I say—you confide rather a lot in your employer, don't you?" Roger put in.

"It's rather difficult to explain. Anyway, he was left with the idea that—that I still saw my ex-fiancé, to use a perfectly horrible expression, only I don't know how else to make it clear. Then when he saw me with you at the ball he thought you were he."

"But didn't this wonderfully observant chap who never misses a detail of anyone's dress, by all accounts, even notice that you called me 'Roger'?" Roger enquired rather crossly.

"Oh, yes, of course. But he didn't know Michael's name, so he still went on thinking you were the man in the case. I'm terribly sorry, Roger."

"Well, considering all the confidential information you seemed to get across to him, I should have thought you could let him know I'm not the confounded idiot who turned you down for Eve Armoor."

"He does know now," Anthea explained rather meekly. "But he didn't at the time when Eve made her spiteful suggestion. He thought she was making hay of my feelings as well as my pride. That was why he coolly turned down the invitation for me, with the information that I was already going to the performance that night with the greatest designer in Paris."

"Yes—I see. Did you tell him afterwards that he'd got your men friends a bit mixed?"

"Of course. It was the first opportunity I had."

"And what did he say?" Roger enquired curiously.

Anthea told him that Florian had muttered that the English were incomprehensible.

Roger laughed at this, and she found she was extraordinarily happy to have his usual good humour restored.

They had a quick, pleasant meal together after that, and then went to a small, nearby cinema which made a feature of showing English films. There, rather crowded together in the back row, they shared that curious, nostalgic pleasure which comes to all those in even the most temporary exile who suddenly see once more a slice of that life which reaches down to their very roots.

It was really not a specially good film, but it portrayed types and used expressions which could belong only to the British. For the first time for many weeks, Anthea felt homesick, and leaning a little against Roger's arm, she was glad that at least she had him here in this lovely, fascinating, but alien city.

They walked home together through the soft night air, past the Eiffel Tower, which seemed to reach away almost to the stars, and along the side of the Champ de Mars, to the street where Anthea lived.

The harmony between them was so complete that after a while he took her hand and swung it lightly as they walked along. She liked the feel of his strong fingers on hers and, smiling a little mischievously—but speaking on a note of satisfaction—she said,

"You're not cross with me any more, are you?"

"Cross with you, Anthea? I was never cross with you." He sounded genuinely astonished.

"Oh, yes, you were. I noticed it because I've never seen you really annoyed before. You were as mad as anything, because I'd let Florian think you were Michael," she reminded him.

"Oh—well——" He evidently recalled the mood, but

125

laughed. "Anyone would be," he declared.

She glanced sideways at him and smiled.

"Why, Roger?"

"I told you. Who do you suppose wants to be confused with a man who could prefer Eve to you?" he retorted lightly. "It's an insult to one's intelligence."

"I see. Thank you."

"Come to that," Roger went on, warming to his subject, "who wants to be taken for a cold-hearted, self-centred sort of cuss like Michael? Why——Oh, I say, I'm frightfully sorry. I forgot for a moment."

"It's all right."

"But I do apologize." Roger looked extremely contrite. "It was a bit tasteless of me to brag about my view of him when yours can hardly be the same."

"It's quite all right," she said again, and blinked her lashes suddenly, like someone who had seen a very bright light.

They strolled on the last few yards together, then he bade her good night, but waited, as usual, until she had opened the big door and stepped into the dimly lighted hall. Then, with a final smile at him, she closed the door and crossed to the lift.

It groaned slowly and reluctantly upwards, as was its ill-tempered wont, but Anthea was too used to it to notice. Besides, she was sunk in thought. Even when she climbed the final flight of stairs and admitted herself to her room, she still seemed oblivious of her surroundings.

"I suppose this is how it comes to one—suddenly," she said aloud. And, without putting on the light, she crossed to the open window and looked up into the star-spangled canopy of the night sky which hung over Paris. "Cold-hearted and self-centred." Those were the words Roger had used. And, as he said them, she knew they described exactly the way she saw Michael now.

The change had come gradually, of course. She had

126

not even noticed that it no longer hurt to think of him. And then that it was no longer a habit to think of him. Only when Roger applied these curt, condemning phrases, she saw that they fitted.

No wonder he had chosen Eve. She was right for him.

And in this final discovery, Anthea realized that the chains of her devotion to Michael had been struck from her.

Eirene twisted another hank of hair. "Accusa... What kind of? What about?" she asked, her tone listless.

CHAPTER IX

ANTHEA opened her eyes and looked at the sunshine pouring in through the window. Then suddenly she remembered it was Friday, and, with a little cry of delight, jumped out of bed.

Today—or rather, tonight—she was to wear the white mink cloak, and go with Florian to the Opéra. Even Paris glowed with fresh colour, scintillated with fresh sparkle, because of it. How infinitely fortunate she was! She, the girl who had walked the Avenue des Champs-Élysées wondering what on earth she was going to do with her life.

And now, in addition, she was even no longer broken-hearted. She was free—free—free! And going to the Opéra with Monsieur Florian. She always came back to that as though it were a recurring refrain.

At work that day she could not altogether conceal her lightness of heart, but she did manage to subdue her very natural sense of gratification at having been chosen for this occasion. To have shown that would have been to invite jealousy, even from those less susceptible than Héloïse. As it was, there were a few oblique references to favouritism. But as Anthea was genuinely very well liked, these were spontaneous and passing, rather than calculated or intentional.

It was Madame Moisant herself who brought Anthea her wonderful green dress, all done up in the familiar striped box which, even now, had sickening memories for her.

"Monsieur Florian will call for you at seven-thirty, and you must be ready then. It is essential that you should be early at the Opéra," Madame Moisant explained firmly. "He will bring the cloak with him."

"I'll be ready waiting in the hall downstairs," Anthea promised. "Does he know where to come?"

Héloïse, who was in the room, permitted herself a scornful laugh at this, but Anthea resolutely ignored her.

"Of course," said Madame Moisant, with a frown which could have been either for Anthea's stupidity or Héloïse's impertinence. "It is in the book, I suppose."

By this somewhat biblical term Madame Moisant did not mean the telephone directory, as most people do, but the register of particulars of the firm.

"Oh, yes—of course."

"Let me see your shoes."

Anthea produced for inspection the lightly strapped silver sandals which she had previously been told to bring from home. These Madame Moisant passed as "possible".

"Gloves and an evening bag you are to have from the *boutique*. The gloves, of course, cannot be returned, but the bag will be," stated Madame Moisant, determined evidently that there should be no silly mistakes about this.

"Yes, *madame*. Thank you." Somehow Anthea maintained her meek and attentive air, though really she could hardly keep from dancing with joyful anticipation.

The day passed at last. The pearl and rhinestone bag had been chosen from the *boutique*, also the perfectly plain but exquisitely elegant white gloves. Still Anthea had seen nothing of Monsieur Florian.

It sometimes happened like this, of course. The whole day would pass without the mannequins seeing anything of him, unless he called one or other of them for special designing or fitting. But, somehow, Anthea had been sure he would say something to her about the evening's arrangements. She had terrible visions of his not being able to find the house, or of their arrangements foundering in some other simple manner, for lack of a little co-ordinating.

However, it seemed that Monsieur Florian was not

tormented by any similar doubts. At any rate, he made no move to get in contact with her, and she went off finally—in a taxi and clutching the dress-box which, this time, she was entitled to carry.

Alone in her own room she once more shook out the cloudy beauty of her green dress and exulted in real ownership at last. But she could not help remembering the terrible night when it had hung there before—stained, dishonoured, and only temporarily restored—the inescapable witness to the crime which should have ended in her dismissal.

Well—things were very different now. This time the presence of Florian himself sanctioned everything that she was doing.

In her anxiety not to be late, Anthea was downstairs in the hall at least ten minutes before her escort was expected. And for half of that time at least, the cross-eyed concierge had a wonderful time peeping at her through the window and obviously speculating on the doubtful path by which Anthea had achieved such magnificence.

When Florian finally arrived, with the white mink cloak over his arm, the explanation was complete. Almost bursting with interest—and personal hopes for the future—she watched while he put the cloak round the insignificant English Miss from the humble top storey. Then she hurried out to wish them both a good evening, and receive from Florian the good, but by no means lavish, tip which established him in her mind for ever as a real gentleman.

Outside stood Florian's large and handsome car, and even his blasé chauffeur paid Anthea—or the white mink cloak—the tribute of a special salute. Then he closed the door, enveloping Anthea and her employer in sudden unfamiliar intimacy, she could not help thinking, and they drove away towards the Opéra.

Florian, looking very distinguished but, as usual, rather worn, leaned back in one corner of the car and turned sideways so that he could see Anthea.

"Yes—it's good," was his comment—she supposed on her general appearance. Then he smiled and said, "You can relax now and enjoy yourself. Do you know *Tosca* well?"

"No, Monsieur Florian, I have never heard it. But Odette assures me I shall like it."

"Of course. Everyone likes *Tosca*," Florian agreed. "Or, if not, they may as well be dead," he added carelessly. "How did you manage to live to your age without hearing it?"

Anthea explained that her father and his circle had been more interested in the stage and the ballet than in opera.

"So? And you had to do what your father did?"

"On the whole, yes."

"And now he is dead?"

"Oh dear, no! He is very much alive," Anthea said, laughing. "He—married again."

"After which there was not the same welcome for the young daughter?" suggested Florian, who could read inflections of speech as other people read words, Anthea had noticed more than once.

"Something like that, *monsieur.*"

"Strange," said Monsieur Florian.

"Not really, *monsieur*. Quite often the second wife is not specially anxious to have a daughter of the first marriage around."

"To be sure. That was not what I found strange."

Anthea wanted very much to ask what he did find strange about the arrangement. But just then the car began to slow down as it joined the long stream of traffic moving up to the great main entrance.

"What a tremendous number of people seem to be going." Anthea looked interestedly out of the window.

"Yes. It is the first time Peroni sings Tosca here."

"Oh?" She glanced quickly back at him. "Then it's the first time you have heard her Tosca also?"

131

"No," he said coolly. "I have heard her do it in Rome."

"And is she very fine?"

"Very."

"I'm curious to hear her," Anthea said, and then wished she had not used the word "curious".

But Florian seemed to think it quite a suitable word. "Of course. It is quite an experience."

Their car drew up opposite the long flight of steps, and Florian handed her out.

"Now, remember that from now until you return to the car you are as much on view as in the salon," he warned her. "Walk slowly up the steps."

Trembling very slightly with excitement, Anthea did as she was told, and, as she slowly mounted the steps and entered the crowded foyer of the Opera House, she was aware of gasps, even exclamations, and those sudden, slight silences which are more telling than any open expression of admiration.

Beside her Florian made one or two casual observations, as though he were completely unaware of the effect she was causing. And, once they entered the building, he greeted several people with a slight, pleasant bow and smile. Among these Anthea recognized his bitterest rival in the dress world. She also noticed that the bow was a little deeper and the smile a little more pronounced on this occasion.

"If you will wait here a moment, I will fetch the tickets," Florian said. And Anthea was left standing at a superb point of vantage at the top of the great staircase.

The "moment" extended to a good ten minutes, and Anthea—who was becoming more knowledgeable about these matters—guessed that the wait had been prolonged on purpose. People did everything but stop short and stare at her. And, by the time Florian returned with the tickets, she was a centre of attraction in what was, in any case, a very well-dressed gathering.

"Come——" He smiled at her, but made no mention of having left her on her own. He took it for granted that, if she did not know the technique by instinct, at least she recognized it when it was presented to her.

Before actually entering the auditorium, he sauntered with her through the pillared promenade, pointing out details of interest. He was a charming and amusing guide, and nothing in his manner suggested for one moment that she was on show. But never in her life had Anthea been stared at by so many people.

She supposed that in the old days it would have disconcerted her. Now she found she frankly enjoyed it. Not only for her personal satisfaction but because the amount of interest she caused was the measure of Florian's success at this moment.

When they entered their box, he said to her,

"Go forward to the front and look round, as though you are interested in the general view of the house. Then turn and stand speaking to me for a few moments."

She did exactly as she was told, aware that the back view of the cloak seen thus must be breathtaking. Then he let her sit down and told her with a smile that she might now enjoy herself.

To Anthea the whole performance was infinitely pleasurable and interesting. But she was aware that her whole attention sharpened and intensified when she heard the first, indescribably musical call of Tosca off-stage—"Mario! Mario!"

Irresistibly, she glanced at the man sitting beside her. But Florian, leaning forward slightly, his thin, rather fine-drawn features clear-cut in the light from the stage, showed nothing but the ordinary interest of any member of the audience just before the *prima donna* enters.

And then Peroni swept in, on a wave of adoring applause—a tall, unexpectedly slender, utterly dynamic creature, with a voice and personality of dark splendour.

Anthea was fascinated. She forgot about Florian and

the personal complications which possibly existed there' and surrendered herself completely to the drama on the stage. That drama which had harrowed, enthralled and delighted so many thousands before her.

Even to anyone of Anthea's small experience, it was obvious that Peroni was a great artist, and as the curtain fell on the first act, she turned enthusiastically to her companion and exclaimed,

"She's wonderful!"

He agreed with a smile, but did not offer to discuss the matter further. And then they went out and promenaded among the dazzling throng—and everywhere they went people looked with interest at the famous designer and the girl with him in the fabulous cloak.

Presently they met Roger and Eve, and since Florian stopped, with a gracious greeting, Anthea had the ignoble—if understandable—pleasure of making Eve look insignificant.

"Everyone is talking about that marvellous cloak." Eve looked at Anthea with ill-concealed envy. "Doesn't it make you feel *odd* to wear something that doesn't actually belong to you?"

"No," Anthea said composedly.

"It does belong to Mademoiselle Gabrielle for the evening," Florian explained coolly. "No one else owns it yet, and so—temporarily it is hers. Perhaps no one ever will own it," he added carelessly.

"What do you mean?" exclaimed Eve, and, to tell the truth, Anthea looked almost equally startled.

"Why, a model of this sort is created for a special occasion, *madame*. It is not necessarily ever sold, unless some very unusual—and, in this case, extremely wealthy —client happens to take a fancy to it."

"Do you mean it is a sort of wildly extravagant advertisement?" Eve asked incredulously.

"One might think of it that way."

"But what other way, if not an advertisement?" Eve pressed.

134

Florian gave that faint, disturbing smile.

"As I said—it is created for a special occasion."

And then the bell rang, and they returned to the theatre.

"I don't quite understand." Anthea spoke softly to him as they re-entered the box. "What is this special occasion?"

"Never mind, *petite*. It is just a manner of speaking. Enjoy the second act. It is in the second act that one has the height of the drama."

She turned her head and looked at him, unable to identify the exact emotion in his voice as he said that. Quiet and expressive as always, the tone curiously conveyed the impression that he was not referring to the actual drama on the stage.

"Has that some particular meaning, *monsieur*?" she asked in a whisper, as the conductor came into the orchestra pit.

But Florian only smiled slightly and did not appear otherwise to have heard the question.

Once more, as soon as the curtain was up, Anthea became absorbed in the action on the stage, following with breathless interest the reactions of Scarpia as he waited for the coming of Tosca. And then again that superb entry—

The gasp which escaped Anthea was echoed by half the people in the house. For the cloak which enwrapped the glamorous Tosca was an infinitely inferior version— a sort of poor relation—of the exquisite cloak Anthea herself was wearing.

Without the glorious comparison, Peroni's costume would have been superb. But almost everyone there had seen Anthea in her memorable glory, either on the stairs or in the promenade or the theatre itself. And there she sat now—well forward in the box, as instructed by Florian—with the light from the stage revealing with pitiless clarity the terrible similarity and the terrible difference.

A curious wave of restlessness and inattention passed over the audience. Too many people were looking away from the stage instead of at it. The centre of interest was shifting—fatally, inevitably—from the drama which should have gripped everyone at this point to the mystery in the stage box.

Never in her life before had Anthea seen a performance killed stone dead before her eyes, but she realized in a moment what was going to happen. And then, very calmly and unhurriedly, she slipped the cloak from her shoulders, turning it back over her seat so that only the beautiful lining was showing.

"Put on your cloak again," Florian said softly but rather dangerously beside her.

"No, *monsieur*. I am too warm," replied Anthea in the same tone, without removing her gaze from the stage.

He made a slight movement as though to replace the cloak.

"No, don't do that," she said, still speaking very quietly, "or I shall get up and go out of the theatre." And she turned her head and looked full at him.

It was a mistake. She was a good deal frightened by the menacing chill of his cold, grey eyes. But something within her—she thought perhaps it was sheer, hot rage—gave her the courage to stare back at him unmoved.

"*Mademoiselle*, it would be much better for you to do what I tell you," he said gently.

"Monsieur Florian," she replied very coldly, "you talk too much, and distract my attention from the opera. Please don't say any more."

Then she turned and looked back at the stage, hoping that he could not see the little tremors of anger and fear which rippled over her.

The act continued. Peroni had the audience completely in her hand again. The cloak was cast aside, forgotten. Nothing mattered now except the music and the drama. Only for one brief moment, after she had

136

killed Scarpia and made her slow exit trailing the cloak behind her, did some people glance again at the stage box. But the attentive girl who sat there in the lovely green dress seemed entirely unconscious of causing any interest.

The curtain fell, the applause broke in waves over the house, and presently the lights went up again.

With a physical effort, Anthea turned to Florian. And because he still looked cold and remote and wrapped away in the fastnesses of his own anger, she said in a tone of quiet rage,

"How *dare* you!"

"*Mademoiselle!* That really is my cue," he said drily, but she thought he was a little shaken by the intensity of her anger.

"I can't tell you what I think of you here, because I couldn't control my voice or my expression sufficiently," Anthea went on. "But afterwards you will explain to me how you came to involve me in such a monstrous scene."

"I am not in the habit of explaining myself to order," Florian said coldly.

"Then you'll break your habit for once," retorted Anthea brutally.

There was a short, astounded silence. Then Florian said,

"Are you coming out for the interval?"

"No."

"You will allow me to point out that you are here to display my cloak."

"I have displayed it," retorted Anthea flatly.

He looked at her again, and she was aware that a faint amusement was beginning to thaw the black frost of his anger.

"I had not realized, Gabrielle, that you could be such a little mule," he said.

"No, *monsieur*? Then perhaps you will now reflect that when a mule kicks it is a very thorough business," replied Anthea.

He laughed at that. A short, angry, rather incredulo◗
laugh. Then he got up and went out of the box, leavi◗
her alone.

She sat there, outwardly serene and calm, making ◗
beautiful and suitable appearance, as she had be◗
taught to do. Even in her anger, she had not forgott◗
his warning that she would be on show until she return◗
to the car. But suddenly, left to herself and aware of ◗
frightful reaction after the tension, she could willing◗
have put her hands over her face and sobbed.

She felt cold all at once, like someone who had had ◗
shock, and she moved to put on her wrap. Then sh◗
remembered and pushed it away again. And at th◗
moment Roger came into the box.

"Oh, Roger!" She only just kept herself from flingi◗
herself into his arms. "Oh, Roger!" She could only s◗
his name, but it was some sort of exquisite relief to repe◗
anything so inexpressibly associated with security a◗
normality.

"All right, darling. Steady on!" Roger sat dow◗
beside her and took one of her cold hands in his. "Ju◗
what is going on here?"

"I—I don't know. Where's Eve?" she counter◗
quickly.

"I've parked her with some American friends of her◗
They're nattering happily, so I slipped away to speak ◗
you. Where's Florian?"

"Oh, I don't know. And I don't care. I think ◗
went off in a rage because I wouldn't go around a◗
more making an exhibition of myself in this thing◗
Disparagingly she flipped a fold of the white mink.

"What was the idea? To humiliate Peroni?"

"And spoil her performance. Didn't you realize ho◗
people started to get restless and look at me and the◗
her, comparing the two cloaks, when they should hav◗
been gripped by her performance? It was an *odio◗*
thing for him to do—whatever she'd done to him."

"Had she done anything specially nasty to him?" Roger enquired.

"I don't know. I don't know anything about him and his horrible private affairs. I only know that no one has any right to try to humiliate a woman or destroy an artist like that. Wild horses wouldn't have got me here if I'd known I was to be used for anything of the sort."

"Well, you dealt with the situation beautifully," Roger told her gently. "Don't be so distressed, my dear."

She bit her lip and made an effort to be calm again.

"I'm sorry. I'm trying very hard not to look as though I'm saying angry or agitated things. It's horrible sitting here on show and feeling like a volcano ready to erupt."

"Poor child." Roger smiled at her in a steady, heart-warming way. "Do you want to go home, my dear? If so, I'll make some excuse to Eve and leave her with her friends for the last act, and take you."

For a moment the prospect of being safe with Roger was so exquisitely enticing that she nearly agreed. Then she remembered the complications this would involve—and, above all, that she would miss her opportunity of some sort of explanation with Florian.

"No, thank you," she said gently. "It's sweet of you to suggest it. But I'll see this thing out now I'm here."

He looked a little doubtful, but she was quite insistent. And presently, with a few more encouraging words, he left her. Just as the lights were lowered Florian returned to his seat.

He and Anthea exchanged no words. Indeed, throughout the last act, they behaved like strangers to each other. And only when the final curtain fell and Peroni, as well as the other singers, had taken her last bow, did Anthea stand up and allow Florian to put the disputed cloak around her.

"I take it you will not come round backstage?" he said, as they went out of the box.

139

"I should be honoured to meet Madame Peroni another time, but not tonight," Anthea replied. And she saw Florian bite his lip—but whether with anger or amusement she was not quite sure.

As they made their slow way to the exit, people stared at her once more, but this time Anthea did not enjoy the experience. Some were still concerned only with the beauty of her appearance, no doubt. But others looked at her because of what had happened in the theatre that night.

When at last they came out to the car, Florian said abruptly,

"Shall I take you straight home?"

"I don't want to go out to supper with you, if that's what you mean," Anthea replied, with a curt ungraciousness she would have thought impossible two hours ago.

"Very well." He gave an order to the chauffeur and got into the car beside her.

Then, as they drove down the Avenue de l'Opéra, Anthea realized that her time would be all too short for explanations if they drove straight to her home and, as though she had some right to speak so to Florian, she said,

"Ask him to drive round a bit, will you, please?"

He gave her an odd glance, and for a moment she thought he was going to remind her that she was the latest and least important of his mannequins. They he picked up the speaking tube and gave the order to the chauffeur.

"That will give us some time to talk," Anthea said, looking straight ahead, rather than at him.

"*Mademoiselle*, very little time is needed for what I have to say," was the dry reply. "I have never allowed open disobedience in any of my staff. Those who attempt to practise it go."

She knew she went rather pale, but she answered resolutely.

"I was not only your mannequin tonight, Monsieur

Florian. In your salon I am entirely at your command. Everyone is aware that we act under orders there. But outside your salon, even if I am wearing your designs, I am a free agent. You had no right to involve me in this scene tonight, to make me your partner in something you must have known I should reject with scorn and loathing if I had known beforehand what was to happen."

"You were there to display my cloak," he said coldly.

"I was not!" She turned on him furiously. "I was there to humiliate your mistress, it seems!"

"Peroni is not my mistress," he stated coolly, and for a moment Anthea was given pause by this categorical denial. But then she rushed on,

"I don't care what your exact relationship is, or what quarrel induced you to do this thing tonight. I only know it was wicked—abominable—to act in that way towards her. But most wicked of all was to involve me—anyone—in it unknowingly. What do you suppose people thought? That I was your next——" She stopped, remembered his denial and changed the wording. "That I had lent myself to this scene because I was so small and mean as to find gratification in being the one who wore the real glory, while she—the great artist—was made to seem inferior and slightly ridiculous. You should have taken Héloïse if you wanted an ally in such an undertaking, *monsieur.*" Anthea gave a furious little laugh. "She would have loved it!"

He was silent for a moment, though he smiled faintly at the reference to Héloïse. Then he said—but without any note of conciliation in his voice—merely as a statement of interest,

"I had no idea you would take this so personally——"

"Then how did you think I would take it?" she demanded.

"For one thing"—again that slight smile—"I didn't imagine you would grasp the implications of the scene so quickly."

"No, of course not! You think I am a simple little

141

soul who doesn't know such things happen, don't you? You thought I'd sit there draped in white mink—so wide-eyed, so unknowing!" Bitterly she flung back at him the words which had curiously moved her when he had used them.

"*Mon enfant*, will you stop berating me for a moment?" There was undoubtedly a hint of amusement in Florian's quietly pitched voice now. "If your rage is based on the idea that people will—misinterpret your position because of this, you are wrong. Alone you might not be recognized yet as my mannequin. With me you were easily identified as the girl who was photographed so much in my wedding dress. Few people will suppose you took any active part in what happened tonight. You were merely the model used for the occasion."

"That isn't the point." But she spoke more quietly now. "I suppose I don't really mind so much what people think, anyway. It—it was the idea that you could use me to stage such a plan."

He gave a slight, impatient laugh.

"Don't you think *I* am entitled to the anger and chagrin there?" he said drily. "Thanks to your disobedience, the plan misfired."

"Oh——" She bit her lip and considered that.

"In fact, since you wrecked the plot and you also say you are largely indifferent to the idea that you personally might be misjudged over this, why exactly are you so angry and distressed?"

It was logical enough. And for a startled moment Anthea reviewed the ruins of her evening and wondered why it was that she still felt cold and shattered and hurt in a way that could be expressed only in anger.

"Well, *mon enfant?*" He watched the varying emotions chase each other across her expressive young face.

"It was—it was—the disillusionment," she said slowly at last.

"I don't understand." He slightly narrowed his eyes.

"I'll try—to explain." She glanced down at her hands

which were gripping the pearl and rhinestone evening bag a little too tightly. "It started as such a radiant, perfect occasion. First that you should have asked me at all—simply to rescue me from Eve's spite——"

"But I told you that it suited me to have you there," he exclaimed a little harshly.

"I didn't entirely believe you, Monsieur Florian." She raised her eyes then and looked at him. "I still felt as though you had—I don't quite know what the expression is—flung the mantle of your protection round me. The—the cloak was almost symbolical."

"You are absurd," he said very quietly, but she saw the hard, thin line of his mouth soften.

"And then—to be wearing the heavenly dress you had given me—without any ulterior motive. Everything about the occasion was generous—generous." Suddenly her voice shook and there was the sound of tears in it. "I was proud to be with you, too. I don't know why I should pretend otherwise. One *is* proud to be with the great unless one is mean-spirited. It isn't a question of vanity. I think I was proud *of* you—the great man, who made occasional gestures of imaginative generosity —my employer—Florian." As she said his name, she began to cry in earnest, the tears suddenly spilling down her cheeks. "And then, all at once, none of it was true at all. It was all calculated and cruel and *un*generous. To the last degree, ungenerous!" And she covered her face with her hands and sobbed.

There was complete and astounded silence in the car except for the hum of the motor and the catching of her breath. Then she heard Florian say softly, incredulously,

"*Mon dieu!* does anyone really care like this about one's feet of clay?" And the next moment he had put his arm round her, and she felt the light, cool touch of his lips against her wet cheek.

143

don't know what came over me to say such horrid
things. Please forgive me. Of course I mind where you
go and what you do.

CHAPTER X

"Don't cry, *chérie*," Florian said at last. "No man is
worth it. Certainly I am not. I had no idea that I could
distress you so much, or I would have been more careful
of you. But—Lord! how was I to know that you
thought me a great man—in those terms? I am not,
you know. I'm a brilliant designer and a successful man.
But I am not great in the high-souled sense."

"Yes, you are—occasionally." Anthea choked back a
sob and spoke without looking up. "You were—the
time I spoiled your green dress, and you bothered to—to
find out the truth about Héloïse—and then gave me the
dress, instead of sacking me for my stupidity, as most
men would have done."

"I couldn't afford to sack you." She knew from his
tone that he was smiling. "I had no one else to put in
your place."

"It wasn't that, really, was it?" She looked up.

"No, *petite*."

"I'm sorry I got excited and cried. It's silly to make a
scene." She drew a long sigh. "I'm all right now." She
sat up, and he immediately took his arm away.

"You have no need to apologize," he said drily. "I
suppose it is for me to do that. If it is any consolation
to you, I did intend at first to take Héloïse tonight. I
made the change only when I heard Miss Armoor being
offensive to you. So far at least I meant well by you.
I am afraid I never thought of your reaction to being
made useful in your turn. I am not used to people who
bother so much about the rights and wrongs of strangers.
I could not guess that you would side passionately with
Peroni."

"Any decent person would!"

"Against me, you mean?"

"In this case—yes. You were in the wrong, *monsieur*."

"It is as simple as that, is it?" He laughed softly. "But you don't really know, do you?"

"What lay behind it all, you mean?" She looked faintly disturbed, as though she might be forced to hear further revelations which she could not bear.

"Don't worry—I am not going to tell you," he said drily. "I have shattered enough illusions for one night, it seems. If you think nothing excuses what I did, the argument is over."

"Monsieur Florian," she said a little timidly, "I am not presuming to sit in judgment upon you. It's only——"

"*Petite*," he said amusedly. "I think perhaps that is exactly what you are doing. But maybe I would rather be judged unheard than explain in unpalatable detail. You might not find it in your heart to weep for me then, and I think I would not have those tears unshed."

"Oh"—she blushed a little—"it was silly of me, I know, but——"

"No, not silly, whatever else it was. I cannot recall anyone else ever shedding a tear about me," he went on musingly. "It is curiously—disconcerting."

She hardly knew what to say to that, so she was silent for a moment. Then, remembering almost the first thing he had said to her after they got into the car, she asked a little apprehensively,

"Am I going to be dismissed—now that we have—talked things over?"

"No," he said with an exasperated laugh. "No, once more you escape dismissal by the skin of your teeth. It is becoming a habit. Are you going to reconsider your decision too and come out to supper with me, after all?"

"Oh——" Suddenly she found that she was hungry and that she very much wanted to go to supper with Monsieur Florian. "But not in this," she said quickly, touching the cloak.

He started to say something, then changed his mind,

apparently, for picking up the speaking tube, he bade the chauffeur drive to the salon.

In two or three minutes they drew up in the silent street outside the deserted building.

"Give me the cloak," he said rather impatiently, and Anthea very willingly slipped out of it.

Taking it over his arm, he got out of the car and crossed the pavement to the entrance. She saw him standing there for a moment, while he drew his keys from his pocket on a long, slender platinum chain. Then he opened the door and went into the building, switching on a few lights as he went.

He was gone several minutes, and she guessed that he was putting the fabulous cloak in a place of safety. She shivered a little without it, but was curiously glad to be free of its ill-starred beauty. And if anyone thought it odd for her to walk into a restaurant without any wrap on a cool spring evening—that was better than to run the risk of some ghastly coincidence in which she might somehow still encounter Peroni while she was wearing the cloak.

She heard the slam of the door, and a moment later Florian got into the car again.

"You had better put this on," he said rather disagreeably. And she saw that he was holding a white velvet evening coat with immense fox cuffs.

"Thank you," she said meekly.

"It is from last autumn's collection," he explained disparagingly, "but there is no need for you to get pneumonia for your principles."

She laughed a good deal at that, and then he too smiled.

"So you can still laugh?" he said.

"Oh, yes—of course. I could even enjoy some supper."

"Good. I feel a little less like a murderer."

"Oh, Monsieur Florian! I didn't really mean to make you feel like that. Perhaps I made rather—rather too much of it all."

146

He gave her an ironical, not unkindly glance.

"Well, one of us got things a little out of proportion. I am not quite sure which," he said. Then he changed the subject entirely, and during the rest of the time she was with him he made no other reference whatever to the earlier events of the evening.

He took her to a small, quiet, exclusive-looking place for supper, where the food was as wonderful in its way as his own creations, and the wine the most exquisite Anthea had ever tasted. He was obviously well known there, and chose everything in that carelessly knowledgeable way that speaks of long experience.

Watching him, Anthea found herself wondering once more about him, and when the waiter had withdrawn and he turned again to her, she said on impulse,

"Monsieur Florian, how long have you been at the top of your profession?"

"About seven years, Gabrielle. And it took me eight to get there," he told her quite frankly.

She started to do some mental arithmetic, but he smiled and said rather indulgently,

"I am thirty-eight, if that is what you are trying to arrive at."

She laughed.

"You are quite generous with your information this evening, *monsieur*. People usually describe you as an enigma."

"The facts I have just given you can be found in any reference book," he assured her. "And I do not claim to be an enigma. I do not know why anyone should describe me as such."

"I suppose," Anthea said musingly, "because so little is known of your private life."

"Anyone who lives in the public eye as I do has practically no private life," he replied carelessly. And then their meal was brought, and there was no further chance to ask about his private life, if any.

Instead, he asked her about her life before she came to

147

Paris, and seemed amused and interested by her description of her father and Millicent.

"And how about the two men in your life?" he enquired amusedly. "What is the situation there?"

"Well, Michael is going to marry Eve, of course. Quite soon, I suppose. But you probably know as much of that as I do. After all, you are making the wedding dress."

"True. You sound cheerful about it. Has it perhaps no longer the aura of tragedy which it once had?"

"Monsieur Florian! How quick you are to notice shades of meaning in one's voice. How did you know?"

"How did I know what?"

"That—that it doesn't matter about Michael any more."

"By—as you said—the overtones of your voice. Besides, your eyes were completely unshadowed as you said his name. It is at least a fair guess that our old friend Time has done his work."

Anthea considered that soberly.

"I didn't know myself until Wednesday evening," she told him.

"No?" Florian smiled. "And what made you know on Wednesday evening?"

"Oh—I don't know.—Yes, I do. It was something that Roger said about him. And suddenly I found that I agreed, although it was rather—rather disparaging."

"Ah—Roger. The other man," said Florian reflectively.

"I don't think I should call him that, Monsieur Florian. At least not in that tone. We are——"

"I know. Only friends," he finished mockingly. "I noticed, however, that friendship extended to his coming into the box this evening and holding your hand while he commiserated with you over the villainy of your employer."

"Oh—you saw that?" She was faintly put out.

"Of course."

She smiled a little and her eyes softened as she remembered how infinitely glad she had been to see Roger.

"He is so awfully nice," she said half to herself.

Florian made a slight face.

"Does he like that description himself?"

"I don't know. I don't think I've ever said it to his face. I suppose he would like it. Why not?"

"It has a certain—worthiness and dullness about it which I find extraordinarily unattractive. I trust you never describe me to anyone as awfully nice?"

"Never," Anthea assured him with such unvarnished simplicity that he looked intrigued—and then slightly nettled.

"Which means that I am not worthy to rank with Roger?" he suggested.

"I shouldn't think of you in the same light," Anthea said gravely. And, though he teased her a little to be more explicit, she refused to be drawn.

He took her home at last, when the ceaseless hum of Paris was dropping to the quietest note it ever achieves. And in the silent, gloomy hall he bade her good night. Even the concierge was asleep by now, and so missed the satisfaction of observing the mysterious fact that the English Miss returned in something less sumptuous than the cloak in which she had departed.

"Thank you for lending me this." Anthea removed the borrowed coat..

"You can bring it to the salon on Monday."

"No. If I do, they will all ask questions," Anthea pointed out.

"Well, you will then be able to tell them the whole story," he retorted rather curtly. "It is not often that one of my mannequins has the satisfaction of outwitting me."

"I have no intention of telling anyone the story, *monsieur*. And it was no satisfaction to have to—defy you," Anthea said gravely.

He looked down at her rather moodily in the half light.

"It took all your courage to do it, didn't it?" he said slowly. "You were very much afraid at one moment."

"Yes."

He put the coat round her again, holding it lightly by the lapels, so that she had to look up at him.

"Will you take the coat and forgive me?" he said, half smiling.

"No, *monsieur*. I will not take the coat, but I will forgive you," Anthea replied with a smile too.

"Why won't you take the coat?" He spoke rather imperiously.

"Because it was enough to take the dress. One does not repeat these things, Monsieur Florian. Or if one does they mean something else."

He studied her for a moment in silence. Then he laughed shortly. "I should like to tell you never to be afraid of me again, *mon enfant*," he said a little sardonically. "But, if I removed the wholesome touch of fear by which I rule you all, I should really have to send you away from my salon. But I promise that never again will I give you cause to cry. Are we friends once more?"

"Of course! And most willingly so." She put up her hands over his for a moment. "Thank you, Monsieur Florian—for everything."

He released her then, bade her a good night as brief and unemotional as if she were Héloïse, and left her.

Anthea was too weary to do more than fall into bed and sleep. But, since the next day was Saturday, she had plenty of time to reflect on the extraordinary events of the previous evening, and to wonder incredulously if they had really happened.

She felt it would have been difficult to credit them at all but for the fact that, among the photographs of notabilities at the opera which appeared in the daily press, there was an excellent one of herself and Florian entering the theatre.

There was some reference to the "fabulous white mink cloak worn by Gabrielle, Florian's latest and most attractive mannequin", but no mention whatever of the drama which the appearance of the cloak had precipitated.

In the afternoon Roger called, with the suggestion that they should motor out along the upper reaches of the river and find some pleasant country inn where they could have an early dinner.

Delightedly, Anthea accepted—remembering, as she did so, how she had described Roger to Florian and thinking that, in spite of Florian's protests, the description both fitted him and adorned him.

"Roger, do you mind being called awfully nice?" she asked, almost before they had started.

"Depends who calls me that." He grinned at her. "Where's the catch?"

"There isn't any catch. *I* called you that. And Florian seemed to think it was a horrid way to describe anyone."

"Well, I can think of some horrid ways of describing Florian, but 'awfully nice' wouldn't be one of them," Roger replied cheerfully. "We use a different measuring rule, I guess. Don't worry. You can call me awfully nice as much as you like, and I'll just purr like a cat."

She laughed.

"Now, tell me—how did the great showdown go?"

"The—— Oh, well, Florian was very mad with me at first for having made his plan misfire. But I talked to him—and he did rather see my point."

"The devil he did!" Roger was amused and impressed. "You must have talked very eloquently."

"I—don't know. I think he was surprised that I was so—hot about it all."

"You mean you just raged at him and he piped down?"

"Oh—no. I suppose I did rage at him, and he just stayed cold and talked about dismissing anyone who disobeyed him. And then I'm afraid I cried——"

"Because he threatened to sack you? The bully!"

"Oh, no. I wasn't worried about that. At least—I mean I didn't really take that in. It was when I was trying to explain exactly why I was so furious and—and miserable about it all. How I'd thought him so wonderful and generous and fine—and then found how abominably he'd behaved."

"Good heavens!" Roger looked at her and gave a protesting laugh. "Are you trying to tell me that you wasted some tears over the discovery that the Florian idol had feet of clay?"

"How odd that you should use that expression." She smiled reminiscently. "He used it too."

"Well, it is the one that comes to mind," Roger said drily. "But do go on. What did Florian do at this point? I should think the situation was without parallel in his varied experience."

Anthea thought of just what had happened, and suddenly she didn't want to tell even Roger about it.

"Oh, I think he was rather ashamed of himself," she explained quickly. "He was really very nice and—more or less apologized for what he had involved me in——"

"I should think so too! Using you to pay off some score against his mistress."

"She's not his mistress, Roger. He told me she isn't—categorically."

"I say—you did take down your back hair, the pair of you, didn't you?" Roger was half amused and half annoyed, she could see. "What else did he tell you about him and Peroni?"

"Nothing. But I said something about her being—that. And he said she wasn't."

"Isn't, you mean."

"Well, it's the same thing."

"No, it isn't. I suppose she was once, but isn't now."

"Oh, I don't think he meant that!" Anthea was a good deal taken aback. "He just said flatly, 'She is not my mistress'—like that."

"Well, there you are! He said nothing about her not

having been so once," Roger retorted triumphantly.

"But the implication was there, Roger. It would have been very—disingenuous of him to put it that way, if she ever had been."

"You'll hardly believe me, Anthea," said Roger, grinning good-humouredly, "but I can quite imagine Florian being disingenuous, as you put it. In fact, with a great effort, I can even imagine him lying like a trooper."

"Not to me," Anthea said before she could stop herself, and then hoped that didn't sound smug.

To her surprise, Roger looked at her consideringly.

"No, perhaps not to you," he agreed unexpectedly. "You're damned difficult to lie to."

"Why, Roger, have you ever tried?" She laughed gaily.

He didn't answer that immediately. And after a moment, she said, on a rather different note,

"You—you didn't ever lie to me, did you?"

"Yes." He spoke with the very slightest touch of bravado. "I did once—pretty thoroughly. I thought the circumstances justified it. I still do. But the odd thing is that I still feel uncomfortable when I look at you and remember that I did it."

"Roger——" She hardly knew whether to laugh or to take him seriously. "I can't image—— Are you going to tell me about it now?" she asked suddenly.

"Yes. Not because I think it would ever be found out. But because I hate having that between us, and I think —I think perhaps the necessity for it is over."

Even then he did not start to explain at once, and from his suddenly sobered expression she thought that perhaps he was regretting the impulse to tell her. But it was too late to draw back now, so after a moment she said,

"When was it, Roger?"

"When we first met. At least, the time you came out with me after the opening show. I didn't want that just to be an isolated incident, and yet I knew that it

153

weighed heavily against me that I was Eve's cousin——"

"Oh, it didn't! I'm not as unreasonable as that," she protested.

"I don't mean that you had a grudge against me for it. But it was perfectly natural that anything or anyone connected with her just made you wince. Left to yourself, you wouldn't have chosen to see much more of me, would you?"

"We-ell—perhaps not. It's difficult now to imagine not wanting to see you again," she said rather naïvely.

Roger laughed. But it was a faintly relieved laugh.

"I knew that must be pretty well how you felt. And yet if I wasn't allowed to keep an eye on you—who would?"

"But did anyone have to?"

"Yes, I think they did, Anthea. You were entirely alone, virtually without money, dependent simply on the caprice of a man like Florian, who might be remarkably glad to have you one week and chuck you out the next."

"I don't think he'd do that," Anthea said gravely.

"You'd be surprised! Anyway, we won't digress to discuss the beauty of Florian's character again," Roger stated firmly. "That was how I saw it, and I darned well meant to see more of you, however I had to manage it."

"Purely as a human duty?" suggested Anthea demurely.

He glanced sideways at her and laughed.

"I wouldn't say exactly that. Anyway, I had to think quickly how I could transform myself into someone you could bear to be with, even though I was closely connected with Eve. So"—again he glanced at her, but a little defiantly that time—"I did."

"I don't undetstand. What did you do?"

"I—maybe it sounds rather far-fetched and officious now—but I thought the only kind of fellow who wouldn't hurt your pride and make you feel isolated in your unhappiness would be one who'd taken the same sort of

154

tumble. You could even feel sorry for him. And there's nothing that does more for hurt pride than to be able to be sorry for someone else."

"Roger! You mean you——"

"Yes." He nodded. "I invented a girl who'd turned me down in similar circumstances. I even gave her a name in my own mind, in case you ever asked for details about her. Fortunately, you never asked very much. I'm not sure that I could have kept it up if you had. As I told you—like Florian, I find it difficult to lie to you."

"But what an extraordinary idea!"

"Are you very angry with me about it?"

"Angry? No, of course not. I was trying to imagine how one could feel so—responsible for an almost unknown girl. Why you should *want* to do such a thing."

"I suppose," Roger said slowly, "it was partly your courage at that confounded dress show. To see both Michael and Eve there must have been the biggest knock you could possibly have taken. And yet no one could have known it from the way you wore those clothes and smiled, and even carried off the scene with the wedding dress. I decided then and there that you shouldn't be left to shift for yourself in the next few weeks or months."

"Oh, Roger, how exactly like you! So that was why you came back and waited for me in the car?"

"Yes. And you thought for a moment it was Michael, didn't you?"

"I'm afraid so."

"You took that shock so well, too, I remember. You didn't want to hurt my feelings, even in that moment. I thought you such a game little thing that I'd have told fifty lies for the chance of getting to know you better."

She laughed at that, and tried—but without success— to recapture her feelings on that occasion.

"Well, I'm glad you told the one lie, anyway," she said quite earnesly. "I don't think I should have agreed to see more of you without it. There was such a relief—

155

such a relaxation—about being with someone who had had all the same experiences, as I thought. I didn't have to pretend, or be brave all the time, or anything. Roger, it was very clever of you." And, with a little laugh, she put her hand for a moment over one of his as it rested on the steering wheel.

"Thank you, darling." He spoke quite lightly, but he turned his hand for a moment and held hers.

"And you were quite right too in thinking that the necessity for keeping up the pretence was over. I don't feel—hurt or humiliated about Michael any more, you know."

"I did wonder—the other night."

"And so"—she laughed again to herself, but rather tenderly, as she thought of Roger's subterfuge—"and so I don't have to bolster up my morale any more by being sorry for someone else, as you put it."

"Good."

"And oh, Roger, I'm so terribly glad that no horrible girl did let you down, after all!"

"To tell the truth, so am I," agreed Roger good-humouredly. "I'm glad to get rid of Cynthia—I called her Cynthia.—It seems to clear the decks completely, somehow."

She laughed over Cynthia and agreed that her removal did "clear the decks". Then she wondered just what they both meant by that term. And slowly the impression began to grow upon her that, in some subtle way, this conversation was bound to change the relationship between herself and Roger.

If he were no longer to be the philosophical fellow sufferer—the companion whose sharing of a common experience entitled him to an unusual degree of confidence and intimacy—just what was he in her life?

Until now, she had allowed herself to think of him almost as a brother. But both her instinct and her common sense told her now that Roger's brotherly phase was over.

CHAPTER XI

ON Monday, when Anthea arrived at the salon, she found herself a subject of interest to a degree that had not existed since she wore the wedding dress at the opening show. It seemed that not only had everyone seen the photograph of her and Monsieur Florian entering the Opéra—enough in itself to excite the proprietorial interest of all on the staff—but also, in some indefinable way, some whisper of the scene inside the building had got about.

Héloïse—naturally the first to broach a delicate subject—looked her up and down with a malicious smile before remarking,

"So you tried to discomfit your rival on Friday night? For publicity some people will do anything."

"What do you mean?" Anthea contrived to look mildly surprised.

"She is sly, that one!" Héloïse laughed scornfully, as she addressed anyone who cared to listen—which, to tell the truth, included all her fellow mannequins. "All Paris knows about it and she says, 'What do you mean?'" She mimicked Anthea's tone rudely.

"It's only a rumour," one of the other girls put in, half apologetically. "But they say that Peroni came in wearing a shabby version of your cloak in the second act, and that when she glanced up and saw you in the stage box, she shook her fist at you."

Anthea laughed—glad to be able to deny at least this with vigour.

"I don't imagine she even noticed I was there," she said. "It was unfortunate about the two cloaks, of course. But how was Monsieur Florian to know she would elect to wear hers on the stage that night? As soon as I realized what had happened, I turned mine

157

back over my chair. I don't think many people noticed. And anyway, she was so marvellous that one didn't think of anything but the performance after a few moments."

Even Héloïse looked shaken, but Anthea saw the very faintest smile pass over Odette's face.

"It is almost unheard-of for Monsieur Florian to duplicate a design of such importance," objected the girl who had retailed the story about Peroni shaking her fist at Anthea. "He *must* have done it deliberately, for some purpose of his own."

"Oh—I don't see why." Anthea shrugged. "I suppose, having designed Peroni's cloak for the stage some time ago, he suddenly thought how beautifully it could be adapted for ordinary wear, in white mink. Anyway, the incident passed off quite well. And I assure you there was no fist-shaking from either of us," she finished with a laugh.

No one said any more just then. If they thought the explanation thin, at least Anthea delivered it with an impersonal firmness that carried conviction. But later, when—Anthea thought with intention—Odette was alone with her in the dressing-room, the older girl took up the conversation again.

"When you turned back your cloak, Gabrielle, what did Monsieur Florian do? Approve?" she enquired, with that faint smile which Anthea had noticed before.

"Well——" Anthea began, in the most plausible manner. Then she saw that Odette, who knew Florian so much better than the others, found it impossible to believe that the whole thing had not been deliberately planned.

"At first he did not approve, Odette. Later, I think perhaps he decided that what I did was for the best," Anthea said.

Odette laughed incredulously.

"I marvel each day, *mon enfant*, how you contrive to remain here," she declared. "What you are really telling me, in your demure way, is that you defied Florian in public—and survived."

Anthea laughed too, but she bit her lip.

"Something like that," she agreed.

"It is not to be understood," muttered Odette. "Unless he is just waiting until he finds a suitable substitute."

"No, I don't think it's that. He did say at first that disobedience meant dismissal. But he—withdrew that later."

Odette looked disturbed.

"Listen, *petite*—I am no Héloïse, with her insinuations and her bad thoughts, but you do realize, don't you, that a man usually makes such concessions only when he expects concessions in return?"

"There is nothing of that, Odette. You needn't worry."

"That is what children think when they poke their fingers through the bars at the lions," Odette retorted. "Well"—she shrugged and sighed impatiently—"sometimes they pull the finger back in time."

Anthea laughed at this graphic way of putting things. But, although she was so calm and confident to Odette, she did feel faintly self-conscious about her first meeting with Florian again after the very personal events in which they had taken part.

She need not have worried, however. He neither avoided her nor singled her out. He merely sent for her, early in the afternoon, to act as model while he made suggestions and experimental designs for the South American girl with the wealthy mother. And, apart from the fact that he did not stick pins in her, Anthea might have been a canvas and sawdust dummy for all he appeared to notice her.

For some reason it faintly piqued her—at least while the recollection of Friday evening lingered with her. But presently she became absorbed in the impersonal identity of Gabrielle, and the fact that she had shed a few tears on Monsieur Florian's shoulder, and been kissed by him, took on an aura of improbability which made it almost non-existent.

Even when Madame Moisant finally escorted the distinguished clients downstairs and Anthea was left alone with Florian, he merely gave her one or two curt instructions, as he might have done to any of the other girls, and then dismissed her with an absent nod, before picking up a pencil and beginning to sketch something which had evidently just come into his mind.

The rest of the week was almost boringly uneventful. Roger was out of Paris on business, which greatly reduced the liveliness of Anthea's leisure hours, while life at Florian's proceeded with such unusual smoothness that Madame Moisant was heard to remark that this must be the lull before some sort of storm.

Anthea was inclined to agree, and she supposed—with the humorous resignation which was becoming her habitual attitude to such matters—that there would be some unpredictable eruption in connection with the immense cocktail party which was to be given in a day or two for the leading lights of the Paris *haute couture*.

This was to be one of those business affairs which disguise themselves so successfully as social events, and half a dozen of the Florian mannequins, including Anthea, were attending, in order to display new designs.

Anthea was looking foward to it as a new experience. Consequently, when, early in the following week, she received a summons to Monsieur Florian's office, her first reaction was anxiety lest something should have jeopardized her attending. A summons to his work-room meant nothing out of the ordinary—merely that one was required for some designing or fitting—but a summons to his office was another matter.

As she reached the door she heard Florian speaking and, when she entered, she found him sitting behind his desk—courteous, unusually relaxed, and playing the host with a faint air of amusement.

"Come in, Gabrielle," he said, as she hesitated on the

160

threshold. "We have unexpected visitors for you." And then, as she came farther into the room, she saw, seated on the other side of the desk, her father and Millicent.

It was a moment of unexpected emotion, in which she discovered that, in spite of all his foibles and weaknesses, her father was the nearest person to her in all the world. He suddenly represented home in a way that brought a lump into her throat and sent her rushing across the room to embrace him. And she even submitted with a very good grace when Millicent bumped a softly powdered cheek against hers in simulated affection.

"Oh, Monsieur Florian—did *you* arrange this?" She was radiant.

But he smiled and shook his head.

"No, *mon enfant*, I can take no credit for it. Your father wished to make his visit a surprise, and since he asked first to see me, I thought it would be best for you to meet in my office."

It passed through Anthea's mind that it was impossible to imagine the fathers of Héloïse or Odette or any of the others assuming that they might call on Monsieur Florian as and when they pleased. But she saw that her employer was amused and not a little intrigued by the situation, so she supposed it was all right.

"Monsieur Florian has just asked if we should like to see the afternoon show," Millicent explained. "It will be very amusing to see you in such a setting."

"Mademoiselle Gabrielle tends to excite admiration rather than amusement," Florian observed politely.

"I'm sure she does," Millicent agreed, opening her fine eyes very wide and turning her most beautiful and compelling smile in Florian's direction. He withstood it admirably.

"But why did you call yourself Gabrielle, child?" She turned once more to Anthea, with rather less of the beautiful and compelling smile. "Why not your own name?"

161

"Monsieur Florian chose Gabrielle."

"One always changes the name, *madame*," Florian explained. "But whether from superstition or etiquette it would be hard to say."

"How quaint! But what made you think of Gabrielle?"

"I think—her likeness to an angel," Florian replied gravely.

"Oh!" Millicent looked as though she thought this excessive. "Her hair, you mean?"

"Her hair—among other things," Florian agreed.

"Well, I never thought of my little girl as an angel," Colin Marlowe said, becoming, however, the father of an angel with great charm and dignity. "But she is a good child," he added, taking full responsibility.

"Yes. She is a good child," Florian agreed with a faint smile. And Anthea wondered why it was that the phrase took on a different meaning when said in that almost gently pitched voice. She was aware that Millicent glanced quickly from Florian to herself.

"Well, Gabrielle"—Florian got up—"you have ten minutes before you need get ready. Stay and talk to your father now, and then take him and Madame Marlowe down to the salon in good time."

Having said which, he bowed to Anthea's father and Millicent, and went out, leaving them in sole occupation of the room to which one only ventured on a very special summons.

"What a charming man!" exclaimed Millicent. "You lucky girl, Anthea—to work here."

"Yes—I think so too."

"Really, he could not have received us more—more cordially. I'm sure I don't know why he should," declared Millicent, while patently attributing the circumstances to her own charm.

There was a certain amount of family competition at this point, however.

"It was the natural courtesy of one artist to another,"

162

Anthea's father explained simply. "For, in a sense, one may call him an artist, I suppose."

"He is a very great artist," Anthea retorted indignantly.

Her father laughed indulgently, which she found annoyed her so much that she hastily changed the subject by asking about their length of stay and their plans while in Paris.

It seemed they were there for a week.

"And our plans are just what we like to make them," her father said. "But they include seeing a great deal of you." And he ruffled his daughter's fair hair and looked effectively melancholy. "I have missed you, child."

"I've missed you too, Father," Anthea assured him earnestly.

"Ah, well, it's different when one is young," her father countered, appropriating the monopoly of nostalgic regrets. "I expect you've been having too gay a time to think much of your old father.

Anthea thought of the desperate hours she had known in Paris. But they were the last thing her father would wish to hear about. So she kept silent about them.

"You must introduce us to some of your interesting friends," Millicent put in. "We can entertain for you while we're here. You won't have been able to do much, living on your own in a poky room. Perhaps you would like to bring Monsieur Florian to dinner at the hotel one evening."

"Really, one doesn't 'bring' Monsieur Florian anywhere," Anthea assured her. "But I'd love to bring Roger Senloe," she added, thinking how pleasant it would be to return some of the kindness Roger had lavished on her.

"Senloe? I don't seem to know the name." Millicent looked reflective. "Is he in the dress world?"

"Oh, *no*! The Diplomatic Service."

"Oh," said Millicent, who apparently put dresses before

163

diplomacy. And then they went downstairs and Anthea found them good places of observation in the salon.

It was not entirely easy playing her part as mannequin before anyone so intimately connected with her as Millicent and her father.

But, by now, the routine was almost second nature to Anthea, and so she acquitted herself quite well.

Afterwards, Madame Moisant herself actually came and made herself very gracious to Gabrielle's parents, as she called them—to Millicent's obvious and intense annoyance. And she explained that Monsieur Florian was seeing to it that they had invitations to the cocktail party which was to take place on the morrow.

"All the important designers will be exhibiting. And a few of no importance whatever," she said a little repressively. "Your daughter will be there, *monsieur*, and I am sure she would like to have you and *madame* attend."

Compliments were exchanged, thanks expressed, and then, rather to Anthea's relief, her father and Millicent took their departure. Since they both obviously regarded her work in something of the light of amateur theatricals, she was happy to see them go before they had made this attitude clear to Madame Moisant.

Roger telephoned that evening to say he was back in town, and Anthea gave him the invitation to come and meet her father and Millicent that very evening. He accepted enthusiastically, agreeing to pick her up in about an hour's time, and Anthea was suddenly and delightfully aware of the feeling of once more being a girl with a background.

She had not actually missed it during the last few months, but, later, sitting at a well-appointed table in a first-class hotel dining-room, with her father acting as host, she could not help thinking that this was all extraordinarily and refreshingly like the old days.

Millicent—always at her best when there was a new and attractive man present—gave a very entertaining

164

account of their visit to the salon, and said again how lucky Anthea was.

"Well, there's Florian's point of view too," Roger said with a smile. "I think he considers he was lucky to get Anthea. She more or less saved his opening show for him, you know."

"Is that why he is so indulgent to her?" Millicent wanted to know.

"Indulgent? I don't think Florian is exactly indulgent to anyone who works for him," Roger said.

"Oh, yes, he is. Calls her *'mon enfant'* and says she is like an angel, and describes her as 'a good child'. If that's not being indulgent, I don't know what is."

"It was *I* who described her as a good child," Anthea's father said rather crossly.

"But not in the same tone," Millicent retorted shrewdly.

"Did he say all that?" Roger looked unusually glum suddenly.

"But it doesn't mean a thing!" Anthea protested.

"Does he call Héloïse *'mon enfant'*?" Roger wanted to know.

"Well—no."

"Or say she's like an angel?"

"No, of course not." Anthea laughed vexedly. "For the very good reason that she isn't. I don't say I am. But he was really only referring to the colour of my hair."

"No. He said 'her hair—among other things'," Millicent recalled with a malicious little laugh. "Good gracious, child, don't apologize! There's not a woman between here and Tonga who wouldn't be glad to have Florian in her pocket. Think of having devotion expressed in terms of Florian models!"

"Oh, Millicent, don't say such silly things!" Anthea found that she was particularly put out to have this conversation take place in front of Roger. "To Florian I am just a satisfactory mannequin, and rather quaint and amusing because I'm more naïve than most of his girls."

"Not naïve, my dear—please," her father protested. "God forbid that any daughter of mine should be lacking in a reasonable degree of worldliness."

This fortunately led to a useful digression about his views on what constituted a womanly woman who yet displayed that reasonable degree of worldliness which he considered so essential. And, to Anthea's profound relief, the subject of Florian was dropped.

But, on the way home, Roger brought it up again.

"Look here, Anthea," he said, as they drove across the Pont Neuf in the moonlight, "I didn't realize that Florian was quite so—so familiar with you."

"He is not in the least familiar with me," Anthea stated firmly. "You mustn't pay attention to Millicent's nonsense. She doesn't understand his particular, almost whimsical way of addressing m—people."

"Does he address Héloïse whimsically?" Roger enquired, rather mulishly, she could not help thinking.

"I don't know why you have to keep harping on Héloïse!"

"All right, then. Does he address Odette whimsically?" asked Roger, making the word seem rather odiously mannered by repetition.

"No."

"Just you?"

"Roger, there is nothing *in* it, I tell you."

"I don't know why I didn't take more notice of all these things before," was all Roger said.

"I don't know why you should want to take notice of them now," retorted Anthea, keeping her temper with difficulty. "You ought to have more sense than to pay attention to Millicent, whose hobby is mischief-making."

"I'm not paying any special attention to her and her views," Roger maintained stubbornly. "Either Florian says and does these things or he doesn't. And then there was that rotten business over Peroni and the cloak. The more I think about it, the less I like it. Anthea— don't jump down my throat for suggesting it—but I wish you'd leave Florian's at the end of the season. You could easily get a job in one of the other dress houses now."

"*Leave*—Florian's? You must be mad," said Anthea. "Why, I adore the place. And, anyway, even if I didn't, how do you suppose I could think of leaving him now? Why, he made me. I'm almost as much a creation of his as one of his own models——"

"Oh, Anthea, really!"

"It's true. I'd be wandering around Paris without a bean by now, but for Florian. Or, worse still, be living on sufferance in Millicent's home."

"Come, it wasn't all Florian," Roger protested. "Madame Moisant made the actual discovery, and your own talent had something to do with it."

"But it was his genius—and, yes, his handling of me— that transformed me. What sort of gratitude would it be, if I went to one of his rivals now?"

"It need not be one of his immediate rivals," Roger said obstinately. "I was thinking of Ormaine's. I could get you an introduction there. You'd almost certainly get a job in their London house."

"I don't want a job in anyone's London house!" exclaimed Anthea, quite enraged at what she considered to be unwarrantable interference in her affairs. "Why should I?"

"For one thing, I'm probably going to be moved to London in a few months' time."

"I don't care where you're going to be moved," retorted Anthea, carried away by her anger. "You can go where you like and do what you like. But I'm staying on at Florian's. Good night."

The opportunity to use this effective exit-line was due to the fact that Roger had just stopped the car outside her home. He tried to protest, as she wrenched open the door of the car and got out. But, refusing to listen to him, she ran into the house without a backward glance.

By the time she reached her room, she had cooled

somewhat, and she was already wishing she had not been so harsh. Certainly she wished she had not said to Roger that she didn't mind where he went or what he did. She minded very much, of course. The thought of Paris without him was not to be contemplated.

But then, neither was the thought of Florian's without herself.

If only she had not pressed the argument to the point of quarrelling. At least—*he* had pressed the argument. But she ought to have been able to argue calmly and without temper. It was inconceivable that she had parted from Roger—*Roger*—in anger. Terribly—urgently—she wanted to make it up with him. But there was nothing she could do now until the morning.

She slept rather brokenly—and then overslept, which made her too late to telephone to Roger before leaving for the salon. In fact, not until half-way through the morning did she have a chance to telephone to his office and then she received the chilling, exasperating reply that "Mr. Senloe was in conference".

After that she had to wait until the afternoon. But this time the reply was even more chilling. "Mr. Senloe cannot be reached just now," the impersonal voice informed her, and for a terrible moment she wondered if Roger had given instructions to reject any call from her. The sheer impossibility of this, however, consoled her on reflection. One simply could not imagine Roger taking offence to that extent.

There was nothing more she could do just then, and it was, in any case, time to dress for the cocktail party. She was to wear a sherry-brown taffeta suit, with a tiny matching hat. The subtle yet brilliant shade of brown brought out the faintly golden tint of her skin, while the twist of taffeta and tulle which was the hat looked like nothing so much as a big tawny brown butterfly on her shining head.

When they were all ready, Florian came in to inspect them before himself departing for the party. He had a

168

brief word for each of them and was, as Anthea had noticed whenever he was likely to meet his fashion rivals, in his pleasantest and most urbane mood.

He paused before Anthea, ran that all-embracing glance over her which, she knew, took in everything from her hat to her shoes, and said,

"Sweet sherry for you, *mon enfant*. If you spill it, it will not show on that suit."

She laughed and blushed a little at this reference to her earlier escapade. But she remembered to thank him for seeing that her father and Millicent were invited.

He acknowledged this with a smile and a slight inclination of his head. Then he went out, while Héloïse was heard to remark that she didn't remember anyone else's parents being invited.

The party was being held at one of the big hotels nearby, and most of the girls walked over. One or two official dignitaries and their wives were acting as hosts and, after a series of handshakes, Odette and Anthea, who were together, passed on into the huge, already crowded room, where everyone had come either to stare at everyone else—in the most discreet manner possible—or else to be stared at.

After a few minutes, Anthea—pleasantly aware of being one of those stared at—found her father and Millicent, the latter frankly enjoying an atmosphere which was the breath of life to her, the former faintly condescending, to indicate that dress-designing was no more than a bastard art, and, as such, not to be taken too seriously by the real artist.

"Hello, Anthea—that's pretty!" Her stepmother regarded Anthea with open envy. "It's exactly *you* somehow."

"It was designed specially for me." Anthea smiled. "The dresses I wore in the show were designed for someone else of my type. But this is individually mine."

"It's perfectly lovely. Where is Monsieur Florian?"

"Oh, he'll be somewhere about. He's one of the distinguished guests, of course, so I suppose he will have to be very sociable."

"We should like to see him and thank him for the invitations in person, however," her father said. And Anthea promised quickly to arrange this if possible.

It was her business to move around a good deal, and so, after a while, she left her father and Millicent and made her way slowly through the room, as though looking for someone. Although she did not admit it to herself, she *was* looking for someone. In her heart there lingered the obstinate hope that she might find Roger here.

Instead, she found Monsieur Florian, who stopped to speak to her and enquire if she had had anything to drink. When she shook her head, he fetched her a glass of sherry and handed it to her with a smile.

"But suppose I don't like sweet sherry, *monsieur*?"

"*Il faut souffrir pour être belle*," he retorted. "The picture is now complete. Are your father and Madame Marlowe here yet?"

"Yes. They hope you will find a moment to speak to them."

"Of course." He bowed and gave his special "one enemy to another" smile as someone passed. "And our friend—Roger?" he enquired. "Is he coming?"

"I—don't think so."

"Not? There were invitations sent to the Embassy and the Consulate. I should think he would manage to get one of them."

Anthea said nothing to that, but she looked suddenly very serious, and after a moment Florian asked quietly,

"What is the matter?"

"*Monsieur!*" She was startled, as so often, by his quick powers of perception. And then, instead of her assuring him that there was nothing wrong, some odd feeling of compulsion made her say, without finesse, "I quarrelled with him last night."

Florian bit his lip—she thought to keep himself from smiling—but his eyes were grave as he said,

170

"I am sorry, *petite*. But to make it up can also be very enjoyable."

"If one—if one gets the chance," murmured Anthea, who felt that she had been trying all day to make it up with Roger.

"Was it such a very serious quarrel?"

"I—don't know. I was very angry, because he wanted me to—to——"

"To what, Gabrielle?" He seemed to be observing the scene all around him, and yet she knew that his attention was completely on what she was saying.

"Monsieur Florian, he doesn't realize how—how devoted I am to my work. He is expecting to be transferred to London later in the year, and he seemed to think that, at the end of the season, I might actually consider leaving you—leaving the salon, and taking a job with one of the London houses."

There was a very slight silence. Then Florian said,

"I see. And you quarrelled about this?"

"Yes." Suddenly she wondered why ever she had been so frank to him, and would have given a good deal to recall her words. But there was no anger or indignation in his voice, only a faint, indulgent amusement, as he said,

"And now you want very much to make it up again."

"Monsieur Florian, I don't like to quarrel with Ro—with my friends."

"Of course not. We none of us do," Florian agreed gravely. "Particularly if we feel uneasily that the other person has been rather reasonable."

"But I don't think he was that!"

"And yet his suggestion was not a bad one."

"Not a bad one, *monsieur*?" She was aghast. "That I should leave you and go to one of the London houses?"

"Since your father lives there and your sweetheart will be going there, I find it reasonable. I should be sorry to part with you, of course——" Suddenly she saw that his attention was now not entirely upon her, but on

171

a remarkably pretty blonde girl who was effusively greeting Odette. "But it would not be impossible to find a substitute for you, Gabrielle, if it is your official conscience which is troubling you."

"I—I was not thinking of that so much. I was thinking that I owe everything to you, Monsieur Florian, and that I should feel terribly—terribly mean if I left you now."

"*Mon enfant*, all my mannequins owe everything to me," Florian retorted lightly, "though few of them admit it. But I am not so unreasonable as to expect them to dedicate their lives to me and my business. Or only at stated times of the year. If you decided to leave me at the end of the season, I should, as I have said, be sorry to part with you. But if it interests you to see your probable successor, there she is, talking at this moment to Odette."

Appalled, Anthea turned slowly and once more gazed at the brown-eyed blonde who was laughing so companionably with Odette.

"I—don't know her," she said, in a slightly choked voice. "Who is she?"

"That is Claudine."

"Claudine?"

"Yes." Florian smiled with an air of rather grim recollection. "The girl who so inconsiderately broke her leg within a few days of my opening show and forced me to make a mannequin of you, *petite*. She is, I see, fully recovered now," he added with professional interest.

And, as though to prove it, the girl turned suddenly and, seeing him, rushed over to greet him, with the utmost grace and good humour.

CHAPTER XII

UNTIL the moment when she saw Florian greet the charming, laughing Claudine with undoubted warmth, Anthea had regarded all the passions and jealousies of the fashion world with something like amused tolerance.

But now, as the two stood there talking together in rapid, friendly, colloquial French, she felt suddenly like the waif outside the window, and she envied—miserably, angrily, uncomprehendingly—she envied the girl who could make Florian laugh so easily, the girl who could apparently supplant herself with complete satisfaction to Florian.

Odette sauntered over and joined the group, and after a moment someone thought of introducing Anthea to Claudine, who explained immediately and generously,

"But she is exactly of my colouring!—Only prettier."

"No." Florian glanced judicially from one to the other. "You perhaps are more obviously pretty, Claudine. But Gabrielle is more unusual."

"You see! That is his charming way of saying I am ordinary," Claudine remarked good-humouredly to Anthea. "Oh, Monsieur Florian! if you knew how homesick I am for the salon. Henri wishes to marry me —now that he has broken my leg," she added, as though this were one step towards matrimony. "But for me he has become inexpressibly boring. And though it is understandable to find one's husband a little boring, to find him quite madly boring is an unfortunate beginning."

"Without doubt," agreed Florian drily. "But, in any case, you would always find marriage boring, my poor Claudine. Permanency and you are incompatible."

"Oh, *monsieur*, how well you understand me!" cried Claudine, almost purring like a cat. "Except that I

173

remain permanently and for ever in love with fashion."

"Ah, that's different." Florian smiled. "Fashion is an ever-changing mistress—or, in your case, I suppose, a lover. It is the most fickle thing there is, always to be wooed, never completely won, fascinating, demanding and completely ruthless."

"Monsieur Florian, how I love to hear you talk again," sighed Claudine. "Henri could not talk this way in a hundred years."

"But then Henri's passion is driving, if I remember rightly," replied Florian.

"True. He has no soul above a carburettor," Claudine agreed. "But then he is very rich," she added almost naïvely.

Florian laughed.

"This also is important," he said. Then, with a little nod which included all three of the girls, he strolled over to talk, with inexpressible charm and cordiality, to a rival designer who would, everyone at Florian's knew, have killed him by inches with the greatest pleasure in the world.

"There is no one quite like Florian," Claudine said, as she turned away with Odette. And Anthea—immeasurably solitary, all at once, in the midst of the crowd—thought, in her turn, "There is no one quite like Florian," and wondered how it was that her world had fallen in ruins.

She should never have told him of what Roger had said —never have given him the remotest idea that she might consider leaving. The suggestion could be withdrawn, of course. She knew too well her value in the salon to suppose that her position was in jeopardy, however eager Claudine might be to return.

But that Florian could himself coolly *advise* her to go—could so calmly and indifferently contemplate her leaving. That was what shocked and wounded her. She could go or she could stay, it seemed. To him it was more or less equal, provided Claudine or another were there to take

174

her place.

That was exactly the impression she had tried to give Roger last night, it was true. She remembered protesting, in front of Millicent, that she was "just a satisfactory mannequin" to Florian. But now she knew that, in her heart, she had cherished the idea that there was a rather particular bond between them. The great designer and the girl he had trusted to save his show. Otherwise, why had he twice reprieved her on the verge of dismissal, and each time with an amused indulgence which surely, surely he had not often used towards a mannequin?

Anthea made her way to one of the deep window embrasures, and stood looking out on to the busy avenue below. She had forgotten that she was on view, or that she was supposed to move around so that people might see her dress. She could think only of the fact that Florian did not really care very much if she worked for him or took herself off to London.

He might even *prefer* to have Claudine back, now that she was available again. And then the waters of the Paris fashion world would close over Anthea, and Florian would look back—if he ever looked back at all—on the brief career of Gabrielle as nothing but an unexpectedly successful stopgap during an emergency.

The very thought brought a lump into Anthea's throat, and, forgetting her professional duties, she turned rather blindly from the window, intending to make her escape from a party which had become detestable.

As she did so, however, she saw a familiar, infinitely consoling figure making his way towards her. Without any trace of chagrin for the parting last night, Roger came up to her and, grinning down at her in a friendly way, said,

"Hello! Are we on speaking terms again?"

"Oh, Roger!" She clasped his hands in both of hers. "If you knew how glad—how glad——" Her voice failed her for a moment. "I'm so sorry about last night. I don't know what came over me, to say such horrid things. Please forgive me. Of *course* I mind where you go and what you do."

"Dear girl!" Roger laughed and held her hand very tightly. "I didn't really suppose you were completely indifferent, you know. I guessed you were just mad with me for the moment because I was tactless."

"Well——"

"I shouldn't have been in such a hurry to spring the idea of a change upon you. But I had only just heard about my probable transfer, and I way busy thinking how we could see to it that the Channel didn't divide us two in the future."

"Yes—I do see." She was smiling a little now. But her heart ached with sudden anguish at the thought that the Channel might divide her from Florian's.

"There is no need to make any hasty decisions," declared Roger—by no means having abandoned the idea of a change, it was evident. "A lot of things can happen in a few months."

"Of course." She smiled again, but more mechanically this time.

"Our business at the moment is to enjoy Paris together," Roger said with a laugh. "Which reminds me— have you seen your father and Millicent yet?"

"Yes, but"—Anthea roused herself determinedly—" I suppose I ought to try to find them again. They don't know anyone else here, and I don't want them to feel out of it."

With her hand still in Roger's—that blessed contact which meant warmth and affection and reliability—she made her way slowly back through the crowd to where she thought her father and Millicent might be. But when she and Roger came in sight of them, she saw that, far from feeling out of it, they were very much enjoying themselves, talking to Florian.

As Anthea and Roger came up, Millicent said something and Florian looked round. That keen, unemotional glance that could take in every detail of an ensemble in a flash did not miss the clasped hands. And, while Roger was greeting the Marlowes, Florian said softly to Anthea,

"So the reconciliation was complete?"

"Yes, *monsieur*."

She also spoke in a whisper, but with lowered lashes and neither smilingly nor intimately. She thought she would never again feel a real bond of amusement or sympathy with Florian. For, with all his charm, he had shown an almost brutal indifference, just at the moment when she felt most loyal and warm-hearted towards him.

She thought he looked piercingly at her, but she refused to look up. And, after a moment, he turned to her father again and said,

"Your daughter tells me that she may seek a position in one of the London dress houses next season. It will be my loss, *monsieur*, but undoubtedly your gain."

"Indeed!" That was Millicent, divided between the practical advantages of having a stepdaughter at one of the London dress houses, and the loss it would be to have not even a distant link with the famous Florian any more.

"Anthea!" Roger exclaimed at the same moment, and looked unusually moved.

"This is very good news, my dear." Anthea's father put his arm round her, with a disregard for the brown taffeta suit which made Florian wince. "You didn't tell us anything about it."

"Nothing is settled yet," Anthea said quickly. "I—I don't want to decide on anything in a hurry."

"None of us would want you to do that," Florian observed courteously. "But in something like six weeks' time, the first plans for the July shows will be made. It would be best for both you and me to know by then if you want to make a change."

"I shall know by then," Anthea said almost curtly, and the subject was dropped.

It was over at last, this party which looked so pleasant and social on the surface, but carried beneath its pleasant exterior innumerable currents of jealousy, rivalry and plain hatred.

Anthea promised to rejoin her father and Millicent at the hotel later, but went back with the other mannequins to change at the salon. They were all talking about Claudine, it seemed, and commenting on her brilliant looks.

"There one sees the real professional," observed Héloïse, who had hated Claudine like poison when she was at the salon. "It makes one realize that the amateur can never be anything but—amateur."

At any other time this would all have slid off Anthea's back. But, unnaturally sensitive as she was after the Florian rebuff, she felt she could hardly bear these comparisons between her and Claudine.

She escaped at last. But even then, she could allow herself only a short respite in the solitude of her own room near the École Militaire. After that, she had to go to the hotel and spend the evening with her father and Millicent. And this, inevitably, meant discussion of future plans.

Millicent tried hard to make her commit herself one way or the other, while her father executed some effective variations on the theme of the lonely parent.

"I expect Florian would be sorry to lose you, in spite of all his polite airs," said Millicent.

"On the contrary, I don't think he would miss me at all," retorted Anthea, making herself smile and shrug indifferently. "He could get back Claudine, the girl who modelled my type of dress before I came on the scene. She was there this afternoon, completely recovered from the accident which put her out of the running before."

"Well, I must say you're casual about your connection with that fascinating creature." Millicent laughed. "But, in any case, it would be a pity to leave before you were quite sure of something else. Having tasted independence and had a place of your own, you would want the same in London, I'm sure."

She evidently meant to make it clear that Anthea must not suppose there was a place waiting for her in her father's house.

"Of course," Anthea agreed coldly. "I shouldn't think of anything else. But I'm not afraid about getting another job. A recommendation from Florian takes one anywhere in the fashion world."

"And then," put in her father, with the air of one who saw further than most, "you may not need even that. I have an idea that Roger Senloe has other plans for you." And he laughed.

"Oh, Father—really, we're just friends," exclaimed Anthea, remembering, as she used the term, Florian's contempt for it.

"But you could be more if you liked just to crook your little finger," Millicent said with a laugh.

Anthea refused to answer that, and managed to keep the conversation on less personal topics for the rest of the time she was there.

But she knew, of course, that Millicent was right. The deep, precious, intimate friendship with Roger could any day become something much more significant.

She sat by her open window, as was her wont, for a long time that evening, gazing out into the warm night sky of Paris, softly flushed with the reflection from a thousand lamps, and she tried to read her own heart and, by it, plan for her future.

Michael had gone from the scene like a half-remembered shadow, and in his place was Roger—solid, dependable, a darling—the stuff of which good husbands were made. She had only to follow out his suggestion and transfer to London when the time came in order to bring that chapter to a happy and inevitable conclusion.

And a very lucky and happy girl she would be, she knew.

To set against that her romantic, inexplicable love for the life she was now living was really rather absurd.

179

She was not a career-girl by nature. She was not a mannequin by passionate desire. She was a girl who, by accident, had come into the crazy, fantastic, faintly unreal life at Florian's. But the spell which the place had put upon her was complete.

The place?—If it were only the place, then any other dress house should do almost as well. There was not so much difference between them. Even in her inexperience, she knew that.

But in all the world there was no other dress house where Florian would come in—worn and impatient, smiling and indulgent, sardonic and amusing, arrogant and brilliant—in any one of the thousand moods which she had learned to watch for and know.

Who else would call her "*mon enfant*" and "*petite*" in just that way? And who else would she wish to have do it?

It was not the life that enthralled her, not even the scene alone that fascinated her. She was captivated by the tremendous, varied, inescapable personality of the man from whom all this stemmed.

And he had told her he that it a reasonable idea for her to leave and go back to England!

Odette had once declared he could be a monster. She had also spoken of his occasional quick cruelty. But Anthea felt she could have forgiven all these theoretical faults, if only he had not been so coolly, monumentally indifferent.

She told herself that her decision was made, and she went to bed and eventually to sleep, thinking that she meant this. But when she awoke next morning, she was as far as every from knowing her own mind. And that day —and for several days afterwards—she went to the salon in a turmoil of emotion and indecision.

Not that anyone suspected this for one moment. She was good-tempered and co-operative with the other girls, obedient and respectful to Madame Moisant, and almost her usual self even with Florian.

In the evenings she went out with her father and Millicent, and gave every appearance of enjoying herself with them. Sometimes they were joined by Roger, and to him she was friendly and almost affectionate, as she had always been. Only she found that, instinctively, she kept their relationship from drifting into anything approaching the romantic. Until she had resolved the chaos in her own self, she must not allow Roger to do or say anything irrevocable.

By the time she came to the last day of her father's and Millicent's visit, she felt that she had been under a strain for long enough. In a way, she was of course sorry to see at least her father go, but there was some relief as well in the knowledge that for them, at any rate, she would no longer have to pretend.

"Well, child, let us know your plans as soon as they are settled," her father said, as he kissed her good-bye. "We shall be very glad to have you back again in London."

He seemed to take it for granted that it was merely a question of time, and that in principle the decision had already been taken.

"If you want me to start looking for a nice little place for you, just let me know," Millicent told her. "I think I know what you would like. But, if I were you, I should think twice before leaving Florian's."

Twice! Anthea felt she had thought two hundred times at least.

But she thanked Millicent, kissed them both, and promised to keep them informed about her plans.

It was a singularly quiet day at the salon, after all that. But in the afternoon she was called to Florian's workroom, where he was busy on the final design for the South American girl's trousseau—the wedding dress itself.

When Anthea came in, he was standing there, regarding several sketches, and on the work-table was a length of soft, iridescent silver tissue. No one else was in the room.

Anthea was used to this kind of work by now. It was tiring, but it was interesting. She stood there patiently, as quite often before, while he tried the effect of the gleaming material this way and that upon her. He hardly spoke to her—hardly seemed aware of her as a person at all. She was a model, so far as he was concerned—no more and no less.

And yet—memory went back to that time he had spoken of her—knowledgeably, indulgently, almost regretfully—the day Odette had accused him of being a *poseur*.

He had said then that she would change, Anthea remembered sadly, and that then he would no longer design wedding dresses for her in the soft, cloudy materials, but in satins and taffetas and tissues.

She glanced down at the material he was draping on her, and on impulse she said suddenly,

"Monsieur Florian, have I changed already?"

"Changed, Gabrielle?" He spoke absently, as he nearly always did when he was working. "In what way?"

"You said—once—that you would not design wedding dresses for me in the more sophisticated materials so long as I was—unknowing, was the word you used. Only when I changed."

"This is not designed for you, *petite*. It is an order for a customer who requires the sophisticated materials. If I were designing for you, the wedding dress would still be in soft and cloudy materials. That is why you will soon have to tell me if you will be here for the next Collection—or in London."

She was silent, but her heart began to beat heavily. And at last she said, with a sort of desperate candour,

"You would rather I went, wouldn't you?"

"I have not said so."

"But you would prefer to have Claudine?"

"I have no feeling in the matter." His voice was suddenly completely empty of expression and, for the first time in Anthea's knowledge of him, flat and un-musical. "I merely think that, in all the circumstances, it might be better if you transferred to London."

Such empty phrases!

"Monsieur Florian," she said, with almost childlike simplicity and distress, "why don't you like me any more?"

"You are mistaken, Gabrielle. No question of liking or disliking enters into this. I only want what is best—for you."

Again there was a short pause.

"Then suppose I say that I intend to stay?" she spoke softly, but with determination.

It was he who hesitated this time. Then he said,

"If I repeat that I think it would be better for you to go, will you please not take that for an expression of dislike."

"Only of indifference." She could not quite keep the note of pain and reproach out of her voice.

"Nor indifference," he replied, standing back to see the effect of what he had been doing.

"But"—she looked fruitlessly for some sign of emotion in the pale, rather set face of the man who—she knew it suddenly—ruled her every thought and action—"if it is neither dislike nor indifference which makes you wish me to go, what is it?"

"I have said—I think it might be better for you."

"Am I not the best judge of that?"

"No, *mon enfant*," he said, and suddenly he looked so disillusioned and weary that she remembered that he was thirty-eight and a man who must have done and seen many things outside her experience in his varied career.

"I don't understand," she told him sadly, and she drooped a little.

"Stand up straight, please. I can do nothing if you slouch like that," he exclaimed, with barely controlled impatience.

She straightened up and bit a lip which trembled.

"*Monsieur*, it is not difficult to see that you truly want me to go. It seems I can do nothing to please you."

"Be quiet," he said harshly. "You know I cannot work if you talk. This is all wrong." And, coming over to her, he flicked the shining material off her and started again.

She swallowed hard and wished she dared to touch him. He seemed so far away in everything but actual fact. But there was a long silence while he worked. Then he stood back, walked the length of the room away from her and said,

"Now—walk towards me."

Some shutter clicked in her brain, and for a moment she was back in that incredible scene when he had first come into the salon and found her there with Madame Moisant.

"That was the first thing you ever said to me," she told him, almost in a whisper. " 'Walk towards me,' you said, 'as though you liked me.' And I did, *monsieur*. And I liked you from that moment. I thought you liked me too, but now you send me away because——"

"My God, do you want it from me in words of one syllable?" he exclaimed, in a tone of supressed passion. "I am sending you away because I love you—I adore every damned thing about you. The way you look at me, smile at me, reproach me, flatter me, berate me, lecture me—— Everything you do is a tormenting joy to me. I love you and I'm fifteen years too old for you, and a hundred years too old in experience. When you were a baby, I probably already knew more of life than you'll ever know. Go home to the life you know, marry your confoundedly worthy Roger, with whom you confidingly hold hands, and remain the happy innocent, unknowing creature God meant you to be."

"But——"

"There's no need for you to explain or protest or even comment. Do you think I didn't see what it meant to you to quarrel with him?—and still more, what it meant to make it up with him? I have not often in my life held my hand when I wanted something, but this time I want someone else's happiness more than my own. I thought I was too cynical—too worldly—ever to drop to such depths of sentiment. But I will even make the final gesture"—and suddenly he gave her his very beautiful smile—"I will make your wedding dress for you, *chérie*. But do not ask me to your wedding."

She had stood where she was throughout this long speech, only once making the attempt to interrupt him. Then, as he smiled at her, she too smiled—the radiant, tremulous, incredible smile which had made his wedding dress famous.

"Florian," she said—and the curious use of this as though it were his Christian name made him go suddenly pale—"when I first wore your wedding dress you told me to look as though the man I wished to marry were there before me. I don't know how I looked—— Darling, I don't know what I have to do, for it isn't make-believe any longer. It's so real—so real—that all the technique is gone—even the words——" She stopped suddenly and just held out her arms to him.

In a second she was in his arms and he was kissing her. Not the light, tender kind of kiss he had given her once before, but quick, passionate kisses that had almost the quality of pain in them. Then he held her a little away from him, looked at her with curiously shining eyes and said softly, "My God, I have not deserved her."

They were probably the only truly humble words Florian ever uttered.

He could not let her go, after that—could not hear enough that she had loved him all the time and not "the worthy Roger" as he insisted on calling his rival.

"Poor Roger—I hope he was not too fond of me," she exclaimed remorsefully. But Florian said with cheerful callousness that someone must always lose.

"At least we never quite reached the romantic stage,"

185

she murmured, her conscience still troubling her.

He looked down at her and smiled.

"You mean I have not many kisses to resent on his behalf?"

"None."

"None? Then he will get over you."

"But would you have got over me, if I had gone with him?"

"You forget, *petite*, that I had already kissed you—once."

"That didn't seem to count much," she objected.

"No?" He laughed softly. "I assure you it was the moment when I was lost."

"Oh—my dear." She leant her forehead against his shoulder, and he gathered her close, silver tissue and all.

"Are you really going to marry me?" He touched her bright hair with his lips. "You know I'm years too old for you, don't you?"

"Not if you love me."

"And that you might well be happier with a better, less difficult man?"

"Are you trying to make me change my mind?" she asked with a smile, and she put her hand lightly against his cheek, as she had longed—and feared—to do only ten minutes before.

"No." He turned his head and kissed the palm of her hand. "I only want you to know what you are taking on."

"I do know," she said slowly. "Believe me, I do know. I am not quite so unsophisticated as you think. I am aware that I might marry a—better, if you like—a more ordinary man, and be pleasantly and uniformly content. I should never know the occasional misery which I may possibly know with you——"

"Oh, no!" he said quickly.

"—but I should also never know the rapture which you alone can mean for me. One must choose, Florian—one must choose. And I have chosen you, my darling—with

186

my eyes open."

He held her then and kissed her—until Mademoiselle Charlotte looked in to ask something, and permitted herself the luxury of a small shriek of surprise and scandalized delight.

"Come in, *mademoiselle*." Florian looked round and addressed her courteously. "Come in and congratulate me. Gabrielle has just promised to marry me, and we shall have to discuss the most important wedding dress this firm has ever made."

Mademoiselle Charlotte came slowly into the room, murmuring her astonished phrases of congratulation. And, in her bright, knowing, already respectful glance, Anthea suddenly saw herself reflected, not as Gabrielle, but as Madame Florian.

There was no question of keeping it a secret after that, even temporarily. It was essential that Madame Moisant should know within the same hour as Mademoiselle Charlotte, unless a major crisis were to be precipitated.

Florian himself came down with Anthea—first to tell the faintly amused and not entirely surprised Madame Moisant—and then to make his own characteristic announcement to her immediate colleagues.

"You will perhaps like to know that Claudine is returning to us," he said, "since Gabrielle will be leaving to become my wife."

There was immediately pandemonium, everyone crowding round Anthea, congratulating, exclaiming, questioning and—already—making suggestions about her trousseau.

For a few minutes Florian stood there with her, smiling, indulgent, indescribably relaxed, as she had never seen him before. Then his secretary looked in to say that he was wanted on the telephone from Lyons and, with a glance at his tyrannical watch, he said,

"I will see you later, *petite*. The South American's wedding dress must wait today. But I shall need you at ten tomorrow. Ten sharp."

187

"Yes, *monsieur*," she said, from force of habit. At which he took her by the chin and kissed her in front of them all, before he went out, laughing a little to himself.

"It is well that he is making an honest woman of you," observed Héloïse, casting her congratulations in characteristic form.

"It is well that you are making a happy man of him," Odette countered. "I have not seen Florian look like that before."

Anthea smiled, but she did not answer either of them. In spirit she was already taking leave of the room where she had known such hope and fear, such misery and joy. Claudine would take her place here again, to laugh and flirt, lounge, pirouette and pose. But none of that mattered any longer. In all that mattered she was now for ever part of Florian's. Her choice was made.

Harlequin

the unique monthly magazine packed with good things for Harlequin readers!

A Complete Harlequin Novel

You'll get hours of reading enjoyment from Harlequin fiction. Along with a variety of specially selected short stories, every issue of the magazine contains a complete romantic novel.

Readers' Page

A lively forum for exchanging news and views from Harlequin readers. If you would like to share your thoughts, we'd love to hear from you.

Arts and Crafts

Unusual handicraft articles are a fascinating feature of Harlequin magazine. You'll enjoy making your own gifts or just being creative when you use these always clear and easy-to-follow instructions.